I've travelled the world twice over,
Met the famous: saints and sinners,
Poets and artists, kings and queens,
Old stars and hopeful beginners,
I've been where no-one's been before,
Learned secrets from writers and cooks
All with one library ticket
To the wonderful world of books.

© JANICE JAMES.

MURDER '97

When Aunt Clarissa gave little Stuart a copy of a book by Horatio Alger in 1897, she could scarcely have known that it would be involved in four murders. If the average detective was handed an inscribed copy of a boy's book fifty years later and asked to trace the original owner, he wouldn't know where to start. However, problems of this sort are meat and drink to Simon Lash, and soon many people are wishing that the mean-tempered detective had never heard of Horatio Alger, little Stuart, or Aunt Clarissa.

Books by Frank Gruber
in the Ulverscroft Large Print Series:

FRANK GRUBER

MURDER '97

Complete and Unabridged

ULVERSCROFT
Leicester

First published in the
United States of America

First Large Print Edition
published October 1995

British Library CIP Data

Gruber, Frank
Murder '97.—Large print ed.—
Ulverscroft large print series: mystery
I. Title
823.912 [F]

ISBN 0–7089–3392–0

Published by
F. A. Thorpe (Publishing) Ltd.
Anstey, Leicestershire
Set by Words & Graphics Ltd.
Anstey, Leicestershire
Printed and bound in Great Britain by
T. J. Press (Padstow) Ltd., Padstow, Cornwall

This book is printed on acid-free paper

1

THE books that lined the walls of Simon Lash's combination office and library hadn't been touched in a week. Lash hadn't been out of the apartment in all that time and he hadn't shaved for four days. For hours at a time he sprawled on the red leather couch, staring at the ceiling. For other hours he roamed through the five-room apartment. He went to bed too early to sleep well and sometimes he got up at three or four o'clock in the morning and smoked a half package of cigarettes and kept Eddie Slocum awake in his own bedroom. Eddie, though, knew him too well to talk to Lash when he was in one of his moods, so very few words had passed between them during the long hours of these days.

On the eighth day, Eddie Slocum came into the office, carrying a book. He found Lash seated on the couch, his chin in his cupped hands, his elbows on his knees.

Eddie said: "There's a man here wants to see you."

"Tell him to go away," Lash replied, without looking up.

"He sounds interesting."

"I said, send him away."

Eddie gritted his teeth and weighed the book in his hand. He was tempted to throw it at Lash, walk out of the apartment and never come back. While he was debating the idea, Lash said:

"How's the bank account?"

"Good enough," snarled Eddie. "Which you know damn well, or you wouldn't be layin' around like this for two weeks without openin' the mail or talkin' to anybody. I turned away four clients this week."

"Well, make it five!"

Eddie Slocum slammed the book to the floor. It skittered to within inches of Lash's feet. Eddie tore out of the room. When he returned three minutes later, he found that Lash had picked up the book and was leafing through it.

Eddie said: "Maybe it's just as well. The guy was crazy. He wanted you to find the kid who owned that book fifty years ago . . . "

Lash looked up. "What?" he asked sharply.

"There's a kid's name on the inside of the book and the date when his aunt gave him the book — eighteen ninety-seven. This nut wants you to locate the kid . . . on'y he wouldn't be a kid by this time."

"Get him back," Lash snapped. "Run outside and bring him back . . . "

Eddie's mouth fell open in utter astonishment. Then Lash roared: "Get him back!" and Eddie leaped to the door. He pounded down the stairs, whipped open the street door and sprang out upon the sidewalk.

"Hey, Mr. Knox," he yelled at a man who was just turning the ignition key in a car parked at the curb. "He wants to see you . . . "

The man shut off the ignition and got out of the car. He was a rather seedy-looking man of middle age, wizened and slightly stooped. He said to Eddie: "Changed his mind, eh?"

"I thought he might, but not so soon.

It was the book that did it. He's a sucker for books, you know."

"That's what I heard."

They crossed the sidewalk and re-entered the door that led to Simon Lash's apartment. They climbed the stairs and going into the combination office and library found Lash still sitting on the couch, looking at the book.

"Mr. Sterling Knox," Eddie Slocum announced.

Lash gave the caller a sour glance and got to his feet. "What's this nonsense about finding the boy who owned this book fifty years ago?"

"I've got the money to pay for it," growled Knox, stung by Lash's tone.

Lash crossed to his desk and went around behind it. He seated himself in the swivel chair but did not invite his caller to sit down. But Knox, scowling at Lash's discourtesy, seated himself on the couch vacated by Lash.

Lash held up the book. "This is a first edition."

"Of course," said Knox.

"You collect first editions?"

"Only Horatio Alger, Jr."

"Why?" Lash asked bluntly. Then, seeing that Knox looked puzzled: "I mean, why should you collect Horatio Alger?"

"Because I read the books when I was a boy."

"So did I, but I grew up," Lash retorted.

Knox pointed to the bookshelves. "I notice you collect Americana and history. Alger's history, too. His books give you a better picture of the sixties, seventies and eighties than you can find in history books. And the stories are about a class of people that are extinct today. Poor people. Proud people who were hungry at times, but who got their food through their own efforts, by their own sweat. They were individualists, those people. They didn't go whining to the government. Sometimes they were exploited by the employers, but they thought that was better than being exploited by mealy-mouthed politicians, because they hoped to become employers themselves. And sometimes they did. They were the people who made this country. They were the only kind of people who *could* have made a country like this."

"Not bad," said Lash, "considering you haven't got a soapbox."

Knox flushed. "All right, I'll cut it short. There's an inscription in that book — "

Lash opened the book and read: "To Stuart, on his 11th birthday, from his Aunt Clarissa, February 2, 1897." He looked up at Knox. "You want me to locate the person to whom this book was inscribed?"

Knox nodded. "Yes."

"Why?" Lash asked.

Knox frowned slightly. "I don't know that I have any reason. Curiosity, I guess. Those inscriptions have always interested me — I get to thinking every now and then, who were those people? What became of them . . . ?"

"And you're willing to spend money — a lot of money — to satisfy an idle curiosity?"

"I spend a lot of money buying books," Knox said testily. Then he gestured to the bookshelves. "And so do you. And you can't tell me you've never been

6

curious about the inscriptions in all those old books."

"Maybe I have," Lash conceded grudgingly. "But not curious enough to spend a lot of time trying to run down one of the people."

"Well, *I'm* willing to spend the time," Knox said, "or rather the money to pay for somebody else's time."

"Just how high are you willing to go?"

"Whatever's necessary."

"This inscription is fifty years old. The book may have changed hands fifty times. A secondhand book is a hard thing to trace; I may run into a dead end."

"They say you can find anybody — or anything," Knox said, "if you try hard enough."

Lash shook his head. "That's not so; they've never been able to find Dorothy Arnold. Or Judge Crater. Thousands of people walk out of their homes every year and nobody ever hears from them. The easiest thing in the world is to lose yourself."

"But this is a book," Knox reminded. "It's a tangible object. Somebody has owned it all during these fifty years. You just have to trace the owners until you come to the original one. A person named Stuart, who was eleven years old in eighteen ninety-seven — "

"He may have died in eighteen ninety-eight," said Lash. "The book may have been sold to the junkman. Try to find a junkman who bought a book fifty years ago . . . " He hesitated. "You want to find just this Stuart? Or anyone who owned *any* book fifty years ago?"

"I want to find one definite person," Knox said.

"But suppose I run into a dead end? You've got other books with inscriptions . . . I could tackle one of those, then?"

Knox shook his head stubbornly. "No, you can't jump around from book to book. You got to pick one certain book and stick to it."

"You picked this book at random?" Lash held it up. "*Ralph Raymond's Heir.* Why not *Ragged Dick*, or *Tattered Tom* — or the *Young Explorer . . . ?*"

"I see you remember your Horatio Alger," Knox said. "As it happens, I have a *Ragged Dick* with an inscription:

8

it's eighteen sixty-eight — which is perhaps too long ago. I decided on *Ralph Raymond's Heir* because the even fifty years appealed to me."

Lash studied the Horatio Alger book for a long moment. Then he exhaled. "Mr. Knox, I'll take the job."

"Good!" cried Knox. "Now let's talk terms. How long do you think it'll take you to run this down?"

"Who knows? But I'll make a flat price for the job. One thousand dollars . . . "

"I'm willing to spend that."

"All right, I may lose money on the deal but that'll be my hard luck. The price'll be a thousand dollars if it takes me six days, or six months — "

"But what if you fail altogether?"

"Then I'm out a thousand dollars. Now, I want to know just two things. When did you get this book and from whom did you get it?"

"I bought it just a couple of days ago from a local rare book dealer, Oscar Eisenschiml."

"I know Eisenschiml."

"He's the man who recommended you. I got to talking with him about these inscriptions and mentioned that I thought of hiring a detective agency some time to see if I couldn't trace a book back to its original owner and he said — "

"All right," Lash cut in, "you've hired your detective."

Knox got to his feet. "About a retainer . . . will you want — "

"Yes," Lash snapped. "I insist that a client get his feet wet. Five hundred dollars . . . "

Knox took out a wallet and after fumbling for a moment, counted out six bills, four hundreds and two fifties. He dropped them on the desk. "You can reach me at the Lincoln Hotel," he said. "I'm retired. Sold out a shoe business in Iowa . . . "

"I'll get in touch with you when I've got something to report," Lash said impatiently.

Knox shook his head and, scowling, headed for the door. Eddie Slocum followed him out. When he returned to the room, Lash was back on the couch, reading the Horatio Alger book.

"What do you make of it, chief?" Eddie asked.

"I'm reading," Lash snapped.

Eddie winced and, getting his hat, left the apartment.

Outside, he walked to Sunset Boulevard, where he caught a bus, and rode down to Vine Street. On Vine he strolled to Hollywood Boulevard and decided to see the picture at the Pantages Theatre. The picture turned out to be two pictures and with newsreel and cartoon consumed three hours.

It was four o'clock when he let himself back into the apartment. And, as he had expected, Lash was still sprawled on the couch. But he was no longer reading. The book was lying open on his chest and he was staring at the ceiling.

Lash said, without looking at Eddie: "Ever read Horatio Alger, Eddie?"

"Not since I was twelve years old," Eddie replied. "He wrote kid stuff."

"That's right, one hundred and seventeen books."

"That's a lot of books."

"More Horatio Alger books have been sold than books by any other author, living or dead."

"Is that good?"

11

"Not necessarily, but a hundred million, more or less, of his books were printed. And almost all of them have disappeared. Worn out, maybe. Or burned, or used as scrap paper to make new books."

"I remember one of them," Eddie said. "I think it was this *Ragged Dick* you mentioned to Knox. It was all about a kid who sold newspapers and found a rich guy's wallet and give it back to him. So then the rich guy gave him a job and in a little while Ragged Dick married the guy's daughter and got all the old coot's money."

"Well, what was wrong with that?"

"Nothin', only I was readin' in the paper last week where a poor cabby found a rich guy's wallet with thirty-five hundred smackers in it and you know what he got for a reward?"

"A hearty thank you."

"Nah, the guy give him five bucks. Imagine, a fiver for findin' thirty-five hundred leaves of lettuce."

"So you think he should have kept the wallet?"

"All I can say is, let *me* find a wallet with thirty-five hundred in it!"

12

Lash picked up the book from his chest and swung his feet to the floor. "Look at this, Eddie."

Eddie crossed the room and reached for the book, but Lash shook his head and pointed to the open pages. Eddie stooped and followed Lash's pointing finger.

He read: "'*You are aware, I suppose, that this is a subtle poison — '*"

"No," said Lash, "read only the words that are underlined in pencil."

Eddie read again: "'*This is poison . . .*'"

Lash turned a few pages, then stopped. "Now read again — just the underlined words."

" . . . '*They have given me . . .*'"

Lash riffled pages quickly. "Again!"

"'*If I die . . .*'" Eddie read.

Once more Lash turned pages and again Eddie read: " . . . '*My cousin, Paul . . .*'"

Then Lash turned pages for the last time and Eddie read: " . . . '*is the murderer . . .*'"

Lash looked up at Eddie Slocum. "How did the whole thing read?"

"*This is poison they have given me,*"

Eddie repeated. "*If I die, my cousin Paul is the murderer . . .* ", He looked blankly at Lash. "What is it, some kind of a game?"

"*I* didn't mark the words."

Eddie's eyes widened. "Sterling Knox?"

Lash shrugged. "Maybe. Maybe not."

"I thought there was something fishy about that guy."

"Then why did you insist I talk to him?"

"Because I only wanted to — " Eddie stopped. He had almost said that he had only brought Knox in because he wanted to rouse Lash from his long lethargy.

Lash said, "I knew damn well that Knox had more on his mind than he told me."

"You think you shouldn't have taken the case?"

"Knox won't put anything over on me."

Eddie suddenly exclaimed, "Say, do you suppose he knew about those marked words and *wanted* you to read them?"

Lash got to his feet. "They still sell erasers for a nickel." He crossed the room and, opening a closet, reached in and got out his coat. He slipped into it. "I'll be back in an hour."

"Where're you going?"

"Down to Eisenschiml's."

"You mean you're going ahead with this book thing?"

Lash made no reply.

2

THE lettering on the window, rather small and away down on the right-hand side, read: *Oscar Eisenschiml — Rare Books — Autographs*. The store was a small one, containing not more than two thousand books.

Eisenschiml was in his early sixties, a rather heavy-set, balding man, with a disposition almost as irascible as that of Simon Lash. He sat behind the ancient rolltop desk at the rear of the store and frowned at Lash.

"A lot of people are collecting Alger these days," he said. "They exhibited *Ragged Dick* at the Grolier Exhibit of the Hundred Significant American Books and it's got so you can't get a copy of the book for less'n a hundred dollars — "

"I'm not starting an Alger collection," Lash interrupted. "I just want you to tell me what you know about this man, Sterling Knox. He said you sent him to me."

16

"He asked me if I knew of a good private detective and I gave him your name. Actually, I know very little about him. Except that he's got money. He came in here two or three months ago and told me he wanted to start collecting a set of Alger. I only had two or three books in the store, but I've been running some ads in the trade papers and I guess I've gotten him twenty-five or thirty books so far. He always pays cash for them."

"How much did he pay for this copy of *Ralph Raymond's Heir?*"

Eisenschiml hesitated. "That's one of Alger's later books, but it's quite scarce for some reason or other. I had to charge Knox twenty dollars for it."

"How'd you get it — through an ad?"

"Either through an ad, or from a book scout."

"Don't you *know* how you got it?"

"Of course I know. I — I got it from a fellow who scouts for me."

"What's his name?"

"The name wouldn't mean anything to you, Simon."

17

"Look, Oscar," said Lash, "I want to talk to this book scout . . ."

"Why?"

"I want to ask him where *he* got the book, that's all." Lash scowled. "And I don't care what he paid for it — or what he sold it to you for."

"Then why do you want to talk to him?"

"I just want to, that's why. Now, are you going to give me the man's name and address, or aren't you?"

Eisenschiml opened a loose-leaf address book on his desk and consulted it. "His name is David Brussell and he lives at eighteen twenty-six McCadden."

"That's just a few blocks from here."

"Yes, but you may not find him at home. He travels, you know, keeps going around to the secondhand bookstores. For all I know he may be in Sacramento today, or San Diego . . ."

"Hasn't he got a phone?"

"No — he's hardly ever home." Eisenschiml frowned. "Now look, Simon, you understand the book business — the *rare* book business; you don't make a lot of sales like you do in a regular book

18

business. So you got to buy as cheap as you can and — "

"I know, I know — and sell for as much as you can. You probably paid two dollars for this *Ralph Raymond's Heir*. That's why you don't want me to talk to Brussell."

"As a matter of fact it was, uh, eight dollars . . . I think."

Lash grunted and left the shop. Outside he walked three blocks westward, then turned north on McCadden. Number 1826 was a small cottage that was sadly in need of paint. He walked up to the door and rang the bell.

A woman of about thirty-five opened the door and looked at him inquiringly. "Is Mr. Brussell at home?" Lash asked.

"Why, yes," the woman turned and called, "David, there's someone here to see you."

A thin blond man came to the door. "You wanted to see me?" he asked in a slight Germanic accent.

Lash showed him the Alger book. "Oscar Eisenschiml gave me your address — he said you were the one who got this copy of *Ralph Raymond's Heir* for him."

"Why, yes," Brussell said. "But I don't understand — "

"I bought the book from him."

Mr. Brussell suddenly opened the door wider. "Excuse me, won't you come in?"

Lash entered a tiny living room. Mrs. Brussell promptly disappeared through a door and the book scout waved to a worn Morris chair. Lash seated himself.

"You're collecting Alger, Mr . . . ?"

"Lash. Yes, I'm trying to get together a set of Alger."

"A very interesting hobby, but Alger books are getting scarce. A few years ago you could pick them up for fifty cents or maybe a dollar, but lately you don't find many of them. And the dealers have gotten smart; they want three-four dollars for the books."

"What did you pay for this one?"

Brussell's eyes fell to the floor. "I don't exactly remember. I buy so many books in the course of a week, you know. Did, uh, Mr. Eisenschiml tell you to ask . . . ?"

"No, he didn't. It doesn't matter. What I wanted to ask you about — where

20

did *you* find this book?"

"Why, I don't exactly remember, Mr. Lash. I buy so many books in the course of a week, you know ..."

"You said that. And you call on a lot of book-stores."

"That's my business. I go around to the stores and look over what they've got."

"An interesting job," Lash said, trying very hard to restrain himself. "But think for a moment, Mr. Brussell, and see if you can't recall where you got the two Alger books?"

Brussell fidgeted uneasily. "I don't see what ... " He cleared his throat suddenly. "Uh, what business did you say you were in, Mr. Lash?"

"I didn't say. But I'm a private investigator — a detective."

Brussell winced. "A detective."

"Don't worry, Mr. Brussell. I'm not after you for anything. It's just — " He opened the copy of *Ralph Raymond's Heir* and held it up so that Brussell could see the inscription on the flyleaf. "These inscriptions have always interested me and I thought, for fun, I'd try running

21

down one of them."

Mr. Brussell brightened. "Say, those things have always fascinated me, too. I get to wondering sometimes who those people were, what they were like. And what happened to them."

"Exactly. And that's what I'm trying to do right now. This inscription is fifty years old, though, and I'm not going to get very far if I'm licked right at the start — if *you* can't remember where you got this book."

"As a matter of fact," the book scout said, "I found it right here in town, a little secondhand store down on Western Avenue. It was on a table with some . . . well, with some bargains." He beamed. "Once in a great while, you find a sleeper. That's what makes this business interesting, you know. I got that book for ninety-five cents. And it's a beauty, isn't it? Worth five dollars, any time." He hesitated, then added, "I let Mr. Eisenschiml have it for three-fifty."

"Good enough," said Lash, although that wasn't what he thought. "But this store on Western Avenue — what's the address?"

"I don't know the exact number, but it's near Sunset — south of Sunset, I mean. On the west side of the street. You can't miss it."

Lash got to his feet. "Thanks, Mr. Brussell."

"Oh, it's been a pleasure, Mr. Lash. And you want I should keep on looking for Alger books for you?"

"Yes, of course. Especially if you can get them at a bargain."

Mr. Brussell smiled and Lash took his departure. Outside he walked down to Hollywood Boulevard and hailed a passing taxicab. Ten minutes later he climbed out in front of a book store on Western Avenue. He told the cab driver to wait and went into the store.

3

TWO or three poorly dressed customers were browsing about. Behind a counter sat a fat, untidy woman. Lash went up to her. "Good afternoon," he said. "A friend of mine told me he bought this book here . . ."

The woman looked at him suspiciously. "I sell lots of books."

"So I imagine. But I'm interested in this particular book and I wonder — "

"What's your friend's name?" the woman snapped.

"Brussell; he's a book scout."

"Oh, him! Yeah, he comes in here right along." She sniffed. "Lookin' for bargains." She reached for the book in Lash's hand. "I shouldn't a let him have this book. I was readin' only today in a trade journal that this is a rare book . . . what'd he charge you for this?"

"A dollar and a quarter," Lash lied.

"I don't believe it."

Lash took the book back from her.

24

"That's what he charged me, but I don't mind his making a profit. He probably paid you only twenty-five or thirty cents."

"I don't sell any books for twenty-five cents. I got good clean books here and I got a nice, high-class trade, see."

Lash shot a quick glance at the shabby book browsers, but nodded agreement. "I'm a newspaperman," he said, "and I'm writing a piece on the secondhand book business."

"Oh, yeah? Well, I can tell you plenty about it. It's a lousy business, see. People come in here and stand around for hours, looking at books and then go out without buying. If I had chairs they'd read the whole books without buying."

"I can imagine. But the angle I'm interested in is, how the dealers, *you* for example, get your books. Take this one. Where did you get it?"

"At the auction, I guess. Lemme see it again." She took the book from Lash's hand again and opened the front cover. "Ninety-five cents, yeah, this was in a barrel I bought about a month ago. All nice, clean books, which is why I marked them ninety-five cents. My best stuff. On'y if I'd a known this was a rare book, that Brussell fella woulda never got it for ninety-five cents, I can tell you."

"What sort of auction was this where you bought the book — rather the barrel?"

The bookseller pursed up her fat lips into a mighty pout. "I tell you, then maybe you go to the auction tomorrow, huh? How do I know you're a newspaperman, huh?"

"You can call up the *Times*."

"Oh, you work for the *Times?*"

Lash nodded. "And what's more, I won't use the name of the auction place — so your competitors won't know about it."

"That's fair enough. Well, it was the Melrose Auction House over on Melrose, near LaBrea."

"I believe I've seen the place. They're open evenings."

"Sure, that's when they sell the fancy stuff. But it's in the morning, early, you got to go to get the junk — like books and stuff."

"Thank you."

Lash left the store and re-entered his waiting taxi. "Melrose, near LaBrea," he told the driver.

It was a few minutes to six when Lash entered the Melrose Auction House. There were only two or three people in the place and nobody was paying attention to them. At one end of the large room a little bald-headed man was seated at a desk, going over some sales slips. Lash went over to him.

"Good evening," he said. "I wonder if I could ask you a question?"

"Sure, why not?" the man replied. "Next sale's at seven o'clock, but if you want to make a private offer on anything in the place — "

"I was sent here by a woman who runs a secondhand bookstore on Western Avenue."

"Mrs. Wekko?"

"I believe that's her name."

"A fat, uh, rather sloppy-looking woman?" The auctioneer nodded. "She's here a lot in the mornings, but she only buys books. Sold her a bunch a month ago, I think it was."

"That's what I wanted to ask you

about. Where did you get the books you sold Mrs. Wekko?"

The auctioneer leaned back in his chair. "You found something in one of the books? People hide the damndest things in them. Money — "

"Not this time. I'd just like to locate the former owner of those books."

"What for?"

"No particular reason."

"Then why do you want to know?"

Lash showed the copy of *Ralph Raymond's Heir*. "As a matter of fact, I'm a book collector — I'm collecting Horatio Alger and I thought I'd like to see if there wasn't another Alger collector in Los Angeles."

"You mean that's a *rare* book?"

"No, not at all. People collect books that aren't rare, you know. In my own case, I just happen to be interested in Horatio Alger."

"Horatio Alger, yeah, sure. I used to read him myself when I was a kid. So that's an Alger book, eh? Haven't seen one in a long time." He smiled. "You can't sell a book individually, you know — the price is too small. Anyway, the kind of trade we get here . . . " He shrugged. "I just dump the books in barrels and sell 'em that way. Two dollars, Mrs. Wekko paid, for a barrel. Cheap, sure, but it'd take all day to sell a couple of hundred books otherwise."

"The source of these books?" Lash persisted.

The auctioneer smiled. "I can assure you that the former owner of those books was not an Alger collector. I doubt if he even cracked open one of those books. A bottle of whiskey, now . . . "

"Who is it?"

"*Was*, you mean. He kept three saloonkeepers going in his time. Jay Monahan, you know. The actor. He died about six months ago and his widow sold the house, unfurnished, and turned over the furniture and stuff to me to sell. Got her a nice piece of change, too. Guess she can use it, because they say old Jay didn't leave her much."

"Mrs. Monahan still lives in Los Angeles?"

"Oh, sure, she's got a little apartment on, let's see, I think it's Harper — "

"Harper!"

"Yeah, here it is . . . " The auctioneer found a card and started to hand it to Lash, but the latter had already seen the number. It was right next door to his own apartment on Harper.

He said: "That address is right next door to where I live myself."

"Is that so? Then you've probably seen Mrs. Monahan, a nice-looking lady of about fifty, maybe fifty-five."

The description would fit any middle-aged woman, but Lash did not tell the auctioneer that. Instead he thanked him and left the place.

At a quarter to seven he finally paid off the cab in front of his own building on Harper — a two-story, white stuccoed place. There was a light in the upstairs window, but Lash merely glanced at it and walked to the next building — which was identical with his own and owned by the same landlord.

The name *Lucia Monahan* was on a card under the doorbell. Lash pressed the button and waited a full two minutes before the door was opened to the length of the chain.

"Yes?" said the woman inside.

30

"My name is Lash — I · live next door."

"Oh, you're the detective?"

"That's right. I wonder if I could talk to you a few minutes?"

The door was closed, the chain taken off and then reopened. Mrs. Monahan, a spry little woman in her middle fifties, looked pertly at Lash.

"I've always wanted to talk to a detective," she said. "Won't you come in?"

Lash stepped into the hall and followed Mrs. Monahan up a flight of stairs to her apartment on the second floor. "I was told that you lived right next door and since I've followed some of your cases in the newspapers I've been very much interested." At the top of the stairs, she suddenly stopped and looked over her shoulder.

"Are you working on a case now?"

Lash said, "Not exactly."

He followed the woman into a room that was a duplicate of his own office and library, but lacked the bookshelves and had mohair-covered furniture.

Mrs. Monahan seated herself on the

couch and Lash sat down on a chair. He said: "I got your address from the Melrose Auction House. I understand they sold your household effects."

"Why, yes," said Mrs. Monahan, somewhat surprised. "I couldn't keep up the big house in Bel-Air, so I sold it and . . . " She looked sharply at Lash. "You know about my late husband?"

"I heard he was an actor."

"He was also — to put it bluntly, Mr. Lash — a boozer. On top of which he had a bad heart and could never get insurance. About all he left me was the house, and that had a mortgage on it. I have enough to live on — if I live in a small apartment like this."

Lash held up the Alger book. "There were some books among your effects — "

"Is that one of them?" A twinge of pain crossed Mrs. Monahan's face. "One of my son's books . . . He was killed on Saipan."

"I'm sorry," Lash said quietly.

Mrs. Monahan leaned back on the couch. Her eyes closed and she seemed oblivious of Lash's presence until he spoke again, when she roused herself.

"I was saying, he probably had this book since the time he was a boy."

"As a matter of fact, I remember that particular book. It was one of two given him by his roommate."

"At boarding school?"

"The military academy. We lived in New York when Jay was in the theatre. Richard attended the Hudson Military Academy for two or three years. At Cornwall-on-the-Hudson."

"How old was he at the time?"

"Oh, ten or eleven. Let me see, no, I believe he was twelve when we took him out. That would be seventeen, no — eighteen years ago. He was twenty-eight when he was — when he was killed."

"And this roommate of his, you don't happen to remember his name?"

"Why, yes, it was Charles Benton; he was a son of Claude Benton, the department store man. Benton's Department Store in New York."

Lash got to his feet. "Thank you, Mrs. Monahan. I won't take up any more of your time."

"Oh, it's perfectly all right, but you've

made me curious, Mr. Lash. Do you mind telling me your reasons for — well, your questions?"

"*My* curiosity, Mrs. Monahan. I wanted to see if it was possible to trace an old book back to its original owner. I bought this book today. The dealer from whom I bought it told me how *he* got it, through a book scout who found it in a secondhand store on Western Avenue. The proprietor of the secondhand store bought it at the auction house and *they* referred me to you."

"And what are you going to do now — get in touch with Mr. Benton in New York?"

"If possible."

"But suppose he doesn't remember where he got the book?"

"Then I'm licked."

Mrs. Monahan followed him to the door. "Mr. Lash, would it be asking too much to let me know how you finally make out?"

"No. I'll be glad to tell you. And thanks again, for helping me."

4

DOWNSTAIRS, Lash walked to his own apartment and, unlocking the door, climbed the stairs. Eddie Slocum was in the office, leaning back in Lash's swivel chair, his feet up on the desk. He was scanning the next day's selections in the *Racing Form*.

He gave Lash a curious glance, but continued with the important job of trying to pick one. Lash, without looking at Eddie, crossed to the desk and picking up the phone, dialed 110.

He said into the mouthpiece, "I want to get New York City; Claude Benton . . . No, I don't know the address, but he's the man who owns Benton's Department Store. A person-to-person call . . . All right, I'll wait."

He hung up and started toward the couch, but halfway there, whirled and headed back for the desk. Eddie Slocum, peering furtively over his *Racing Form*, removed his feet hastily from the desk and sprang up from the chair. Lash seated himself in it.

Eddie said: "Get anywhere?"

"I've traced it back eighteen years. Only thirty-two more to go."

Eddie was surprised. "You think you *might* lick it?"

"I'll know after I talk to Benton. The trouble with this is that I might get down to forty-nine years and then lose it. A sale to a junkman anywhere along the line would stop me. I've got my fingers crossed."

The phone rang and Lash scooped it up. "Yes? . . . Speaking . . . " He waited a moment, then: "Mr. Benton . . . ? You don't know me, but my name is Simon Lash. I'm a private detective . . . No, no, no one's in trouble. My case is a rather peculiar one. I'm trying to trace a book through its various owners and I've learned that this book was owned, eighteen years ago, by your son Charles — isn't it? . . . The book? Oh, it's just a boy's book — a Horatio Alger book, called *Ralph Raymond's Heir* . . . I don't imagine you remember it yourself . . . " A gleam came into his eyes suddenly, and he listened for a moment. "Mr. Benton, do you recall where *you* got the book?" He stopped again and frowned. "That's the point I really want to know, Mr. Benton. I'm sorry you can't remember, but look, it's rather important. Do you suppose you could telephone me if it occurs to you sometime during the next day or two? . . . Simon Lash, Granite two, one-one-two-seven, Hollywood, California. Thanks very much, Mr. Benton . . . Oh — by the way, where is your son today? No, no, no reason, it just occurred to me . . . Thanks. Thanks very much. Goodbye . . . "

He hung up and exhaled heavily. He began shaking his head slowly as Eddie Slocum waited for him to announce the result of his conversation. But when Lash lapsed into a brown study, Eddie could stand it no longer and exclaimed:

"For the love of Mike — spill it!"

"Spill what?"

"What Benton told you!"

"Oh, why *he* gave the book to his son. It was one of his own books that he had from the time he was a boy. But he can't remember where he got it."

Eddie groaned. "Then you're stuck!"

"If he can't remember where he got the book — yes." Lash picked up the phone again and dialed the long distance operator. When he got her, he said: "Operator, I want to get Charles Benton at Las Vegas, Nevada. That's the C–B Ranch, near Las Vegas. A person-to-person call. Yes, thank you."

He put down the telephone, got up and went to the bookshelves. He took down a thick volume, entitled *Who's Who*. He turned the pages, found the entry he wanted, then read aloud: "Benton, Claude L., Merchant. C. L. Benton & Co., New York City, N.Y. Born Mt. Miller, Illinois, June eleven, eighteen eighty-nine. Parents, Edgar C. Benton and Maria Hoopston . . . " He read silently for a moment, then nodding, closed the book and returned it to the shelf.

"Eighteen eighty-nine," he said. "Kids usually start reading Alger at the age of eleven or twelve and read him until they're about fourteen, maybe fifteen. That means he could have gotten the book anywhere between the year nineteen hundred and nineteen hundred and four — "

Eddie exclaimed, "That's getting close, Simon."

Lash nodded. "I'm back between forty-three and forty-eight years. And I'm in Mt. Miller, Illinois. Now, if Benton would only remember *where* and *how* he got this damn book . . . "

The phone rang again and Lash caught it up. "Yes? Speaking . . . " He waited a moment. "Mr. Benton? I was just talking to your father in New York. He told me where you were . . . My name's Simon Lash. That's right, I'm a detective. No, nothing serious. I'm tracing the original ownership of a book — a book you owned and gave to your roommate, Richard Monahan, when you both attended the Hudson Military Academy — a Horatio Alger book, called *Ralph Raymond's Heir* . . . You didn't . . . ? Well, that's not important. The point is, your father told me the book was one of *his*, that he had from the time he was a boy. He gave it to *you* . . . I'm not trying to verify anything, I'm just trying to trace the original owner of the book . . . " A flash of anger suddenly twisted Lash's face and he slammed the receiver on the hook. "He hung up," he said to Eddie Slocum. "Couldn't be bothered." He scowled at the telephone. "Spoiled pup!"

"Well, that's that," said Eddie Slocum.

"I'll be damned if it is."

"But if Old Man Benton doesn't remember where he got the book you're through, aren't you?"

"I am not. There's still Mt. Miller, Illinois. It said in *Who's Who* that his father was a blacksmith. That means he was in modest circumstances and his son wouldn't be running to Chicago or other towns to buy books."

"I think you got something there," said Eddie. "So he probably got the book in Mt. Miller."

"I'll find out tomorrow."

5

EDDIE SLOCUM was pouring the coffee the following morning when the door buzzer sounded off.

"Oh-oh, before breakfast," he said, and putting down the percolator left the little kitchen. Simon Lash rescued the toast from burning and was buttering a slice when Eddie returned to the kitchen.

"There's a wild man here," Eddie announced. "Says his name is Benton — "

"Junior or senior?"

The kitchen door was slammed open and Charles Benton stormed in. He was a lean, dissipated-looking thirty and at the moment wore an expensive, wrinkled suit. He needed a shave.

"So you're Lash," he said in a rasping voice.

"So you're Benton," Lash retorted. "The brat who hung up on me last night."

Benton's slightly bloodshot eyes widened. "It's going to be like that, eh?"

41

"If you've got any silly idea that your old man's money is going to intimidate me, you can save yourself a lot of trouble by getting the hell out of here right now."

Benton grinned wickedly. "This is gonna be fun. Did you read in the papers what happened to the private dick my ex-wife hired to shadow me?"

"I don't read the papers," Lash snapped, "and if I did I'd skip anything about a sap like you." And with that Lash kicked back his chair and sprang to his feet.

Benton was two or three inches taller and several years younger, but he stepped back at the savageness of Simon Lash. He said: "Hold it. I flew here from Las Vegas to talk to you. I want to know why you're trying to dig up that old scrape between young Monahan and myself."

Lash gave Benton a contemptuous glance and brushed past him through the swinging door into the library. He let the door swing shut in Benton's face, but Benton followed him and was a little less belligerent when he reached the library.

42

Lash said: "I don't know what you're talking about."

"I'm talking about Monahan and myself. We had a fight at the Hudson Military Academy and he broke his leg when he fell down the stairs."

"You mean you threw him down the stairs?"

"He slipped and fell."

"All right, he slipped," Lash said testily. "But I don't give a good goddamn if he slipped or you threw him down. I'm interested in exactly what I told you last night on the telephone — a book. And that's all."

"Monahan swiped that book from me."

"Sue him."

Benton blinked. "How can I — he's dead."

"Sue his estate."

"For a ten-cent kid's book?"

"Well, you're the one that's complaining."

Benton regarded Lash sullenly. "I wasn't complaining about the book."

"Then what are you beefing about?"

"You. I want to know why you're butting into this thing."

"I told you twice."

Benton exclaimed, "If you expect anyone to believe that, you're crazy."

"Don't say that again," Lash warned.

"But it isn't reasonable . . . a private detective trying to find out who owned a book fifty-sixty years ago."

"I don't pick my jobs, they come to me."

Benton pounced on that statement. "That's it — *that's* what I want to know. Who's paying you for this job?"

"That's something you'll never know," Lash said coldly.

"We'll see about that," Benton snapped. He pulled out his well-filled wallet. "How much is this client paying you?"

"Enough."

"Every man's got a price," sneered Benton. "What're you getting? A hundred dollars?"

"Do I look like a dime-store clerk?" Lash demanded indignantly.

"All right, so you're getting more. Maybe five hundred. *I'll* give you a thousand for the name of the man who hired you." And Benton began skimming out hundred dollar bills.

Lash looked at the money as rage mounted within him.

Benton held out the sheaf of bills. "Just the name of the man who hired you!"

"Get out of here," Lash said thickly. "Get out of here before I take that money and shove it down your throat." He started for the young millionaire.

Benton's mouth twisted into a sneer. He took a half step sidewards and his right fist drew back. He was all set for Lash's advance, but Eddie Slocum came hurtling out of the kitchen, leaped past Lash and grabbed Benton's wrist. He twisted the arm around and behind Benton and forced the younger man to yelp in pain. The hammerlock bent Benton over.

"Let me go!" he cried.

Eddie Slocum propelled him quickly to the door, opened it with his free hand and gave Benton a shove that sent him halfway down the stairs before he could recover his balance. From that position, Benton turned.

"I'll get you for this," he snarled. "I'll get you both."

"Write us a letter about it," Eddie Slocum retorted.

Benton continued down to the foot of the stairs. He jerked open the door and collided with a woman who was standing there, pressing the door buzzer. In his anger, Benton did not even apologize to the woman.

She stood in the doorway, looking up at Eddie Slocum. "Is this Mr. Simon Lash's office?" she called up the stairs.

"That it is," Eddie replied.

The woman started up the stairs and as she came closer Eddie saw that she was really quite young, not more than twenty-three or four. And a very attractive young woman, too. But Eddie remained at the head of the stairs, blocking her entry into the apartment itself.

The girl stopped a couple of stairs below Eddie. "Isn't he in?" she asked.

"That depends. What'd you want to see him about?"

"Why, I understand he's a private detective."

"That's what it says in the telephone book."

"Well, isn't he — a private detective?"

"Yes."

"Then I want to see him."

She took another step up the stairs, but Eddie remained immovable and she exclaimed in annoyance, "I want to see him on business."

Eddie shook his head. "He's got a case now. He never takes two at a time."

"This won't interfere with anything he's doing," the girl persisted. "I merely want him to find a book."

"What?"

"A book — I want him to find it for me."

Eddie stared at the girl for a moment. Then he said: "Come," and turning, went into Lash's library, where Lash was now seated on the edge of the red leather couch.

Lash looked up as Eddie came in with the girl.

"The lady wants you to find a book for her, boss," Eddie said shortly, and continued on into the kitchen.

Lash got to his feet and regarded the girl sourly. He didn't like pretty girls.

She said: "You're Mr. Lash?"

"I'm not Clark Gable."

47

The girl's lips twisted in contempt, but she was determined to see this thing through and held her temper. She said: "My name is Nell Brown."

"Not Green? Or Black or White? Just Brown?"

"It's my real name," retorted Nell Brown. "And I've gone this far and I'm still with you. I want to employ you to find a book for me — "

Lash looked at her suspiciously. "What kind of book?"

"A juvenile book, a — a book that belonged to my brother. It's one of those Horatio Alger books you hear about all the time."

"The title wouldn't be *Ralph Raymond's Heir*, would it?"

She seemed surprised. "Why, yes. But — but how did you know?"

"I guessed," Lash said sarcastically. "Horatio Alger wrote only one hundred and seventeen books, so I guessed that *Ralph Raymond's Heir* would be the one book you want."

She looked at him sharply and did it very well. Even her tone seemed genuinely puzzled. "But how could you

48

make a guess like that — one title in a hundred and seventeen?"

Lash exhaled wearily. "The man we threw down the stairs, just as you rang the bell — guess what *he* was here about?"

"How should *I* know?"

"He was here about a Horatio Alger book and don't guess — let me tell you; it was *Ralph Raymond's Heir.*"

Her eyes widened in astonishment. She even took a step or two backwards. "But that's absurd!"

"Isn't it?" Lash asked wickedly. "And you want to know something else? There was somebody here yesterday about that book, too. What do you think of *that?*"

She saw a chair and stepping to it, sat down abruptly. "I don't know what to say."

"I could throw you down the stairs," Lash said, "like the last one who was here about the book."

Nell Brown shook her head in bewilderment. "I don't understand it. I just don't understand it at all."

"That makes two of us who don't understand it."

"You — you said somebody was here *yesterday* about — about this Alger book . . . Who . . . was it?"

Lash chuckled. "Just like that, eh?"

"What do you mean?"

"You think I'm going to tell you the name of a client?"

"I was only wondering . . . "

"I know. You were only wondering."

The girl drew a deep breath and looked steadily at Simon Lash. "I hardly know what to say."

Lash said bluntly: "You've said that. Why not try telling the truth?"

"But I have — I mean, I *did* tell you the truth. I came here to employ you to find a book for me."

"All right, and maybe I'll take the case. But if I do you're going to tell me some things first. Why did you come to *me?*"

"You're in the telephone directory."

"So are the names of twenty other investigators."

"Perhaps I read about you in the newspapers."

"My name hasn't been in the newspapers for six months."

"But you were in six months ago."

Lash shrugged an admission and the girl went on, more confidently, "And it was a case that involved books."

"All right," Lash growled. "Let's skip that one, for the time being. Now, why do you want this Alger book — *Ralph Raymond's Heir?*"

"That," Nell Brown said firmly, "is something I'm not going to tell you."

"Good," Lash said. "I didn't want your case anyway."

The girl got suddenly to her feet. "As you said, there are twenty other private investigators in this town and one of them ought to be civil to a client."

She headed for the door. With her hand on the knob, she hesitated as if expecting Lash to stop her. But he didn't and she went down the stairs.

Eddie Slocum came out of the kitchen. "No soap?"

"This is getting to be an interesting case," Lash said.

"What's interesting about it?" exclaimed Eddie. "I was listening from the kitchen and if you ask me that dame was lying like hell."

"That's why it's interesting. Young Benton lied — and so did Sterling Knox. I think I'll run over and let Mr. Knox lie to me some more." He grunted. "At least, *he's* paying for his lies."

He went to the closet and got his hat. Then he left the apartment and walked over to Hollywood Boulevard, where he caught a bus that deposited him in front of the Lincoln Hotel a few minutes later.

He entered the hotel and approached the desk. "Mr. Sterling Knox," he said to the clerk.

"Use the house phone," the clerk replied loftily.

Lash went around to the side of the desk and picked up the house phone. "Mr. Sterling Knox's room."

A connection was made and after a moment a voice said: "Yes?"

"Mr. Knox?" Lash asked. "This is Simon Lash; I'm down in the lobby."

"It's a very nice lobby, as lobbies go," retorted the voice on the phone.

Lash was in no mood for humor. He gritted his teeth. "What room are you in? I want to talk to you."

52

"About what?"

"The book."

There was a short pause. Then the voice on the phone said: "What book?"

"You're Sterling Knox, aren't you?"

"Yes, of course. What'd you say *your* name was?"

"Simon Lash."

"And what's that about a *book?*"

Lash said grimly, "A Horatio Alger book."

There was another pause. Then the voice said: "Look, Mr. Lash, it so happens that I own a few Horatio Alger books, but so help me, I never heard the name Simon Lash."

"I'm beginning to believe that," Lash interrupted. "Unless you've changed your voice since yesterday. That's why I think I'd better come up to your room."

"All right, the number's eleven hundred and five."

Lash went to the elevators and a moment or two later stepped out on the eleventh floor. The door of Room 1105 was nearby and it was standing open.

6

LASH knocked on it as he entered the room, which he saw was actually a bedroom, living room and kitchen apartment for permanent guests. A heavy-set man with iron-grey hair got up from the sofa.

"Mr. Lash?"

"Yes," replied Lash, "but you're not the man who came to my office yesterday."

"Of course not. I never laid eyes on you before now. You say someone who called himself Sterling Knox came to your office yesterday?"

Lash nodded. "About an Alger book."

The heavy-set man pointed to a narrow three-tiered book rack. "I've got quite a collection of Alger books. My hobby."

Lash walked to the bookcase where some fifty or sixty books were stacked. He looked moodily at the books. "Is there a copy of *Ralph Raymond's Heir* here?"

"Why, no, for some reason or other that's one of the rarer Alger books. Although it's one of his more recent ones. You've got a copy, Mr. Lash?"

Lash nodded. "Yes."

"A first edition?"

"It looks like one. It's published by the Lupton Company . . ."

"That's it," Sterling Knox said earnestly. "What do you want for it?"

"I'm sorry, I can't sell it."

"Why not? You're in the book business, aren't you?"

"No."

"But you said this — this man who gave you my name came to see you about a book."

Lash said bluntly: "I'm a detective, Mr. Knox. A private detective."

Knox stared at him in astonishment. "Say, what's this all about?"

"That's what *I'd* like to know. A man who gave his name as Sterling Knox came to see me yesterday. He brought with him a copy of this *Ralph Raymond's Heir* . . ." Lash's eyes suddenly narrowed and he crossed to the telephone. He picked it up and said: "Hempstead one, five-one-one-five." Then a moment later: "Oscar, this is Simon Lash. Tell me — this Horatio Alger book buyer, is he a wizened old duck between fifty-five and sixty? . . . I see. One thing more — how'd you deliver the copy of *Ralph Raymond's Heir?* . . . Thanks." He hung up abruptly.

"That was Oscar Eisenschiml. He described you correctly, but he said you sent a messenger to his store with the money for *Ralph Raymond's Heir.*"

"I never did anything of the kind!" exclaimed Knox. "This is the first I even knew he had that book."

"Eisenschiml said he sent you a card."

"I never received it."

"Of course not. It was intercepted by someone here at the hotel."

"Who'd do a thing like that?" cried the real Sterling Knox. "And what'd be the point? *Ralph Raymond's Heir* isn't *that* valuable."

"Your double paid twenty dollars for it."

"Which is just about all it's worth."

"As a matter of fact, Eisenschiml got it for three and a half and the scout who

56

got it for him picked it up at ninety-five cents."

Knox grimaced. "That's the book business for you."

"This man who passed himself off as you," Lash said, "he's crowding sixty, about five feet ten and weighs something like one-forty. He's slightly stoop-shouldered. Know anybody looks like that?"

"No," replied Knox, "but that description could fit hundreds of people. I certainly don't know anybody like that out here in Hollywood."

"Where're you from, Mr. Knox?"

"Illinois."

"Mt. Miller?"

"Why, yes, how'd you know?"

"I'll tell you in a minute. You're a retired businessman?" And as Knox nodded, "That wouldn't have been the shoe business, would it?"

Knox stared at Lash in amazement. "How could you know that if you didn't even know me . . . ?"

"I know the *other* Sterling Knox. And he apparently knows you, for he gave me your biography — as his own, of course."

"Then he must be from around Mt. Miller, Illinois, because I don't know a soul in California. I only came out here a few months ago — after my wife died."

"By the way, Mr. Knox," Lash said casually, "isn't Mt. Miller also the home of the New York department store man — " he snapped his fingers, as if trying to recall the name.

"Claude Benton?"

"Yes. You know him?"

"I haven't seen him in more than thirty years, but we went to school together."

"He's done all right."

Knox grimaced. "I'm not exactly waiting for an old-age pension myself."

"Didn't I read in *Who's Who* that Benton's father was a blacksmith?"

"That's right. Us kids used to hang around his shop. The old man was a card. Drank like a fish and tough — he could swear like eighteen mule skinners."

"Make a lot of money?"

"Old Benton? When he died there wasn't enough money to bury him. Claude had to quit school. He was only about thirteen or fourteen at the time."

"He's a self-made man, then? A — Horatio Alger success?"

"With a little help from *my* father. He gave Claude a job in his shoe store. We still did a retail business then. In fact, I didn't start manufacturing shoes until I had the store for five-six years. Claude had moved away from Mt. Miller by that time. Chicago. He started as a stock boy in one of the department stores there." Knox suddenly grimaced. "But what's all that home-town history got to do with this Alger book?"

"Not a thing, Mr. Knox. Not a thing."

"This fella who's passing himself off as me — I got a good notion to report him to the police."

"What's he done — aside from getting a book that you should have gotten?"

"I dunno, but he might start writing out checks in my name."

"Then you'll have something on him. I don't think beating you out of a book would exactly come under the heading of grand larceny and the Los Angeles police are awfully busy these days — getting traffic violators. They don't have much time for anything else."

Knox rose to his feet. "Tell you what I'd like you to do, Mr. Lash. When this fellow who claims he's me comes back to you, wish you'd hold him in your office and give me a buzz on the phone. I'll run over and see who he is."

Lash made no promise, but shrugged, which could mean anything. Then he took his departure.

Down in the lobby, he sought out the bell captain, a balding 'boy' of about forty-five.

"Like to talk to you," Lash said.

"Go ahead."

"Privately."

The bell captain regarded Lash impassively. "Not this week, the heat's on."

"No gambling," Lash said, "no horses, no women. Information."

"I'll meet you downstairs, outside the barber-shop," the bell captain said. "In about one minute."

Lash found the stairs to the basement, entered the washroom and washed his hands. When he came out, the bell captain was just descending the stairs.

Lash took a five dollar bill from his pocket and handed it to the bell captain.

60

The latter stowed it away. "Shoot."

"You've got a guest on the eleventh floor," Lash began, "Suite eleven hundred and five."

"Farmer from Iowa."

"Illinois," Lash corrected, "and he isn't a farmer. He's a retired shoe manufacturer. Well-heeled."

"He gave me a nickel two weeks ago and all I did was run to the drugstore for him — the one over on Highland Avenue, because they don't carry his brand of stogies next door."

"You're making up for it now. Anyway, somebody got some of his mail, a skinny, wizened bird crowding sixty. Stoop-shouldered."

"Sounds like my uncle."

"Does he stay here at the hotel?"

"No, he lives in Santa Monica. I just said this guy sounds like my uncle, only it wouldn't be him."

Lash frowned in annoyance. "How's the mail distributed here?"

"It's put in the boxes."

"The guests call for it, then?"

"Unless they call the desk and ask for a boy to bring it up to them." The bell captain pursed up his lips in a mighty purse. "What's the angle, chief? Anybody can give me five bucks, but five bucks is five bucks."

"How much is ten?"

"That depends. I make over ten grand a year and it ain't a tough job, if you know what I mean."

"In other words you like your job?"

"Keno!"

"This isn't going to get you into any trouble. What you tell me goes in one ear and it stays there. There's nobody here but us. You can deny anything."

"Well, I don't know what you're talking about, but this is a hotel, a *big* hotel. We got fifteen-twenty permanents here up in the apartments. But most of the guests come and go. We don't try to know them all. Say you get yourself a room here for the night and in the morning you pick up the phone and you say to the desk, 'This is Joe Doaks in Room eleven hundred and five. Is there any mail for me?' And then the clerk says, 'Yes,' and you say, 'Will you have a boy bring it up to my room?' Okay, so I send a boy up with the mail, or maybe I take it up myself. And

I meet the guy in front of the elevator and he says, 'Are you bringing up the mail I just called down for?' So I give it to him, see?"

"Yes, I see," said Lash, "but Sterling Knox is a permanent guest; you know *him* by sight, don't you?"

"I didn't say anything like that actually happened, did I? I said, it *coulda* happened. All right, this Knox is a permanent, but he ain't been here so long and he gives nickel tips, so maybe the guy who gets his mail ain't Knox, but what's a postcard and a couple of circulars? Maybe the bellboy knew Knox, but figured the other guy was a pal of his, maybe visiting and picking up his mail to give to Knox. So what? Who cares?"

"Nobody," Lash said, "nobody except me. And I've got twenty dollars says you couldn't find me the name of the skinny guy who *might* have been given the wrong mail on say, the morning of June sixteenth."

"Twenty bucks is interesting money," said the bell captain, "but if the guy ain't here no more I wouldn't know how to go about finding his name."

"He registered when he was here," Lash said, "and he probably had a room on the eleventh floor, too. You could eliminate the women and the regulars and those who had the rooms then and still have them. And the remaining names wouldn't be so many . . . "

"Yeah," the bell captain conceded, "there might be something to what you say. Tell you what, go in the barbershop and let the boy shine your shoes. I'll page you in ten or fifteen minutes."

"The name is Lash."

The bell captain nodded and went off. Lash re-entered the washroom and washed his hands once more, then went into the barbershop and got his shoes shined. He was just stepping down from the stand when the bell captain came into the shop and called out: "Paging Mr. Lash."

"That's me, son," Lash said.

"Telephone, sir."

Lash left the barbershop with the bell captain. Out in the hall the latter took a slip of paper from his pocket. There were three entries on it. They read:

Nicholas Geller,
   San Francisco, Calif.   –1122
O. J. Halpin,
   Chicago, Illinois   –1106
Hugh Tannen,
   Salt Lake City, Utah –1114

"My name's Halpin," Lash said.

The bell captain nodded in agreement. "I think you're right. The room's right across from eleven hundred and five and I'm almost sure that the guy I gave the mail to — I mean, the guy that had that room was a skinny old gazabo. I'll take that twenty in one bill."

Lash gave it to him in two bills, but the bell captain made no protest. He said: "I never saw you, I don't know anything about any mail that was given to the wrong people."

He headed for the stairs and took them two at a time. Lash followed more leisurely. In the lobby he started for the elevators, but before he reached them changed his mind and went instead to the public telephone booths. He entered one and dropping a nickel, dialed the number of his apartment.

"Anything new, Eddie?"

"Yes," exclaimed Eddie Slocum. "In fact, I just called Eisenschiml to see if you weren't there. Sterling Knox telephoned and said he was coming over. He ought to be here any minute."

"Hang onto him," Lash snapped. "Don't let him out of the place until I get there."

He slammed the receiver back on the hook and hurried out of the hotel. Outside he stepped into a taxi.

7

FIVE minutes later he climbed out in front of his apartment and saw a taxicab just disappearing around the next corner. He let himself in the door and hurried up the stairs.

The phony Sterling Knox was just seating himself as Lash entered the library. "Oh, hello, Mr. Lash," he said. "I thought I'd drop in and see how you were getting along on that little matter."

"I'm getting along fine," Lash growled. "Despite the fact that you lied like hell."

The pseudo Sterling Knox reddened. "That's kinda rough talk."

"You'll hear rougher in a minute. What did you tell me your name was?"

"I told you it was Knox, but there's no law says a man has to use his own name all the time, is there?"

"There's a law says you can't take the name of a real person with intent to defraud."

"Defraud? Me . . . ?"

"And the government doesn't like people taking other people's mail — even postcards, Mr. Halpin."

The client relaxed in his chair. "I see, Mr. Lash," he said. "I didn't make a mistake coming to you. You're sharp." He shook his head. "And I suppose you spilled the whole business to Sterling Knox?"

"I spilled nothing, except that somebody's been using his name — to get a Horatio Alger book."

"Well, now, about that book, Mr. Lash — "

"What about it?"

"It seems to me I gave you some money, quite a lot of money, to try to locate the original owner of that there book."

"You didn't tell me to locate the original owner, you told me to give you the name of the original owner — not his present whereabouts."

"Naturally I meant that, too. I want to find the person who owned the book, this Stuart something or other . . ."

"Why?" Lash asked.

"Because I'm curious — that's why. I told you that."

"You also told me your name was Sterling Knox."

"All right, so I gave you the wrong name. You don't give your real name everywhere, do you?"

"Where are you staying?"

"That ain't important, Mr. Lash. I'll call you from time to time."

"There won't be anything to call me about," Lash said grimly, "unless you tell me the truth about yourself."

"But you know it now. My name's Halpin, Oliver Halpin."

"And you're from Chicago?"

"Uh, Mt. Miller."

"What business are you in, in Mt. Miller, Illinois?"

"I'm retired."

"But not from the shoe business."

"No, uh, I was in the dried milk business."

"When'd you get into that?"

"Always was in it. I mean my father had a dairy and I changed it over to a dried milk business. But don't you go telling Sterling Knox about me. We

69

never got along when we was kids."

"How'd you get along with Claude Benton?"

Oliver Halpin's eyes flickered for a moment. Then he said: "Knox told you about Benton?"

"I talked to him on the phone last night. You see, *he* owned the Alger book, forty-five years ago."

"You're sure of that!" cried Halpin. "I mean — you *traced* it to him?"

"It wasn't so hard. The last private owner was Richard Monahan, the son of Jay Monahan, the actor. Young Monahan was the roommate of Charles Benton, Claude's son, at military school. He got the book from young Benton, who in turn got it from his father. Claude tells me he had the book from the time he was a boy. That would be at least forty-three years ago, and possibly as long ago as forty-eight."

"That's swell, Mr. Lash," Halpin said eagerly. "Now who did Claude get the book from?"

"I haven't learned that yet. Claude can't seem to recall. Maybe *you* can help me there. How old is Claude Benton?"

"He's a couple of years younger than me, let's see, that would make him about fifty-eight."

"So, in eighteen ninety-seven he was eight years old. Too young to read an Alger book. Mmm, his father died when he was thirteen and he had to go to work at once. Which means that he wasn't probably spending money for books. So we've run it down to nineteen two, definitely. And I'm quite sure we can get three years on the other end, as no one would be likely to buy an Alger book for anyone under ten. That gives us a three-year span — eighteen ninety-nine to nineteen two. Claude Benton got the book sometime during those three years. Now — Mt. Miller is a rather small town, isn't it?"

"The population's under two thousand today and forty-five years ago it didn't have half of that."

"So there probably wasn't any bookstore in the town at that time?"

"Oh, no, there ain't one there today."

"What are the closest towns?"

"Oregon, six miles away, but that ain't

much of a town either. Freeport's a city, though — that's twenty-five miles away and Rockford's about thirty."

"Fair-sized places. Dixon would be around there too."

"Yes, she's only twelve miles away. But Dixon's smaller than either Freeport or Rockford."

"Any bookstores there?"

"Today — or forty-five years ago?"

"Forty-five years ago."

"I don't remember. I doubt it. You must remember, in those days twelve miles was a big distance. You didn't drive that far in a horse and buggy."

"You could go by train."

Halpin smiled. "You don't know Mt. Miller. There's no train into the town — no passenger train, that is. The main line of the Burlington passes through Oregon, then there's a six-mile branch line shuttles over to Mt. Miller, but it's mostly used for freight. In the old days you had to take a stage-coach from Mt. Miller to Oregon and then to Dixon — a pretty big trip. And roundabout. These days there's a bus to Oregon, but none to Dixon . . . "

"A jerk town, I take it?"

"It ain't even a whistle stop, because there's no train goes through."

"Then how did people buy books in Mt. Miller fifty years ago?"

"The same way they still do — from Sears Roebuck and Montgomery Ward."

"Mail order companies don't sell secondhand books."

"Well, there you got me. I don't know how anyone bought a secondhand book in Mt. Miller fifty years ago. But did it have to be *bought?*"

"Not necessarily; it could have been given — or stolen."

"That's what I was thinkin'."

"Look, Halpin," Lash said suddenly, "you've been beating around the bush long enough. Now tell me, was there a boy in Mt. Miller named Stuart . . . ?"

"You mean fifty years ago?" Halpin shook his head. "I don't know. That would make him sixty-one years old today — a year older than myself. I'd know him if he lived in Mt. Miller in eighteen ninety-seven."

"And you didn't know anyone named

Stuart then — or now?"

Halpin hesitated for just a moment. Then he shook his head. "No."

Lash said suddenly: "How about a woman with the name of Clarissa?"

"My mother's name was Clarissa." But as Lash showed sudden interest, "Only I know doggone well she didn't have any nephew named Stuart."

"Halpin," Lash said, "just how badly do you want this information?"

"I paid you five hundred dollars, didn't I?"

"And how much more are you willing to spend?"

"As much as I have to — within reason, of course."

"Would you go to three thousand?"

"I might."

"And just for curiosity's sake?"

Halpin spread out gnarled hands. "Look, Mr. Lash, some people spend their money collecting old beer mugs. Some of them play horses. *I* collect books."

"Do you?"

"What do you mean — do I? I said I did, didn't I?"

"You bought *one* Alger book."

"I've got fifty-sixty of them at home."

"Have you a copy of *Now Or Never?*"

"There's no Alger book by that name."

Lash strode to his desk and picked up the copy of *Ralph Raymond's Heir.* "You've read *this* book, Halpin?"

"I read it when I was a kid."

"Not since then?"

"No."

"Do you remember the story after all these years?"

"I remember most of the Alger stories that I read as a kid. This one's about a boy whose father's poisoned by his nephew. The will appoints the nephew the guardian of the boy and the guardian takes the boy out to the Middle West, where he tries to get rid of him. Only the boy escapes . . . and in the end he gets back his money."

"That's reasonably close, as I recall the story."

"You read it?"

"Yesterday. I also read it when *I* was a boy."

"I didn't think they were reading Alger when you were a kid."

"I got in on the tail end of his popularity. They don't read him today." Lash seated himself at his desk, opened the copy of *Ralph Raymond's Heir* and said casually: "Mr. Halpin, who is Nell Brown?"

Halpin looked puzzled. "Is she someone in an Alger book?"

"No."

"Then I don't know her. Leastwise, I never heard the name. Why do you ask?"

Lash waved away the question. "You're not going to tell me why you *really* want to find Stuart?"

Halpin exclaimed peevishly, "You've got a one-track mind, Lash. I've told you over and over that I haven't got any reason — except curiosity."

"And I've told you over and over that I don't believe that."

"It's still my money I'm spending," Halpin said grimly. "The question is, you want to continue, or you want me to get some other detective?"

Lash weighed the copy of *Ralph Raymond's Heir* in his hand. "Oh, I'll continue. I may have some more

76

information tomorrow. Where can I reach you?"

Halpin chuckled. "Not at the Lincoln Hotel."

"Suppose I've got to get in touch with you in a hurry."

"There won't be any hurry. I'll telephone, or drop by."

Lash shrugged.

Halpin went to the door, opened it, then turned back. His mouth opened as if he were going to say something further, but then he changed his mind and went out.

The moment the door was closed Lash pointed to it. Eddie nodded.

"Just a minute, Eddie," Lash said, "did you follow the Brown girl?"

"Yeah, sure, the Oro Grande Apartments; it's a dump on Orange, right near the Roosevelt Hotel."

"Good."

Eddie went down to shadow Oliver Halpin and Lash pulled out a drawer of his desk and took out a loose-leaf book. He turned the pages, then finding the entry he wanted, picked up the telephone. He dialed a number.

"I want to get Chicago," he told the long distance operator. "Wells eight-three-eight-three."

He held onto the phone as the operator got Chicago in a matter of seconds. Then he heard the Chicago operator ring Wells eight-three-eight-three and a moment later a whining voice said: "Sam Carter talking."

"Los Angeles calling," the operator said. "Just a moment, please."

Lash said: "Sam, this is Simon Lash."

"Jeez!" exclaimed Sam Carter. "All the way from Los Angeles, huh?"

"Shut up, Sam," Lash snapped, "this is costing me money."

"It'll cost you more if you want me to do anything. I'm in the middle of a mighty big case — "

"Then what the devil are you doing sitting in your office? Now listen, I want you to run down to a jerkwater place called Mt. Miller — "

"It ain't down," cut in Sam Carter, "it's out. About a hundred miles west — "

"Stop interrupting, Sam! Wherever the hell it is, I want you to go there — right away."

"But I told you I was in the middle of a — "

"Then drop it. I'll pay you more."

"Okay, if that's the way you feel about it, but — "

"Write down these names," Lash said angrily. "Claude Benton, Oliver Halpin and Sterling Knox. Got them? . . . Good! These men are all between fifty-seven and sixty or sixty-one years of age and the first left Mt. Miller a good many years ago. Anywhere between forty and forty-five years ago. I want to know everything about these men — especially what they did as kids. What trouble they got into, etc. And I want to know about their families . . . And now, write down these names — Stuart, Clarissa. Those are given, not family, names. I don't know their last names, but Stuart was born February second, eighteen eighty-six. Clarissa was his aunt. Now get this — I want to know what happened to Stuart shortly after February second, eighteen ninety-seven — his eleventh birthday. I want to know if he died. And oh — he had a cousin named Paul but whether or not Paul was Aunt

Clarissa's son I don't know, but look into it . . . You got all that . . . ?"

"I got it, Lash," exclaimed Sam Carter, "but holy cow! Do you know what you're asking me to do? Enough work for sixteen — "

"Cut it out, Sam! Fifty years ago Mt. Miller was a spot on the prairie; it didn't have five hundred people. But they probably had a town clerk — or maybe a newspaper. That work oughtn't to take you more'n a few hours."

Sam Carter howled, but Lash interrupted him savagely. "Stop yelling and get at it. I want you to leave for Mt. Miller right now — within five minutes after I hang up."

"All right, Simon, but I've got to charge you — "

"How much?"

"Well, you're making me drop this big case — "

"Cut it out — how much?"

Sam Carter gulped. "Five — I mean, a thousand dollars . . . "

"Five hundred!"

"All right, but better wire me a hundred to Mt. Miller. It's too late to get a check

80

cashed and I've got just about enough on me to get there."

"I'll wire the money. And look — the minute you get something — anything hot about any of the people I mentioned, call me . . . "

"I'll burn up the wires!"

Lash hung up and stared at the telephone a moment. Then he exhaled heavily and pushed back his chair. He paced up and down two or three times, then suddenly went to the door and descended to the street.

Outside he walked to the adjoining apartment building and rang a doorbell. After a while the door was opened the length of the chain and Mrs. Monahan peered out.

She brightened at sight of Lash. "Oh, Mr. Lash!" She closed the door, removed the chain and reopened the door. "Won't you come up?"

"I won't take your time Mrs. Monahan. I just want to ask you a question . . ."

"Of course. But tell me, have you already — "

"No," Lash said, "I'm getting along, but I don't know the answer as yet. But tell me — when your son attended the Hudson Military Academy . . . did he break his leg?"

Mrs. Monahan hesitated.

"Why, yes, he did."

"Was it an accident . . . ?"

Mrs. Monahan hesitated again. "I was a little afraid you'd find out about that. As a matter of fact, it *wasn't* an accident. He was *pushed* down the stairs — "

"By Charles Benton?"

She nodded. "Benton was suspended from the Academy and — well, you might as well know the whole story. We — I mean Jay, insisted on suing Benton, Senior. And we — I mean, he finally made a settlement." She cleared her throat. "Five thousand dollars. That was many years ago, you understand, before — before Jay came to Hollywood. We *needed* the money in those days. But I — I always regretted the incident. Young Benton, I understand, was pretty much of a bully, still . . . " She sighed. "There *were* witnesses."

Lash nodded.

"Thank you, Mrs. Monahan."

"It's all right," she said listlessly.

Lash turned away and she closed the door. He continued up the street, past his apartment to Sunset, then beyond to Hollywood Boulevard, where he waited for a few minutes and then got into a bus.

8

A SHORT while later he got out of the bus in front of the Roosevelt Hotel and went down a side street.

The Oro Grande Apartments turned out to be an ancient mansion that, having fallen upon sad days, had been converted into an 'apartment' house. It still looked like an old mansion, however, in need of much repair and paint. A sign outside read: *Oro Grande Apartments*.

Lash went up to the front door, found it open and entered. Inside was a wide entry hall and a staircase leading to the second floor. There was a series of mailboxes in the hall and Lash consulted them. The name Brown was not on any of them, but Lash had not expected it to be.

He stepped to a nearby door and knocked on it. There was no response and he went to another door. The door was opened, after he knocked, by a

84

blowsy woman in her forties, wearing a dirty, flowered wrapper.

"I'm looking for Miss Nell Brown," Lash said.

"There's nobody here by that name," the woman retorted. "And I think you got a crust going around banging on people's doors . . . "

"I'm from the Hollywood Credit Association and I want . . . " Lash stopped, for the door was slammed in his face.

He returned to the mailboxes and consulted the names once more. While he was looking at them, he heard footsteps on the porch and, looking out, saw Nell Brown just approaching the door.

"Well," he greeted her, "fancy meeting you here."

She gasped in alarm. "H-how . . . ?"

Lash grinned sardonically. "I was just looking for your name on the mailboxes. It isn't."

She backed away from the door. For a moment, it seemed that she would turn and run away, but then she faced Lash, her chin coming up an inch or so.

"What do you want?"

"Not much. Just your real name?"

"That's none of your business."

"All I've got to do," said Lash, "is ask anyone in this house . . . and make you an object of suspicion."

"You wouldn't . . . !"

"Oh, no?"

She bit her lower lip. "I guess you would, at that. But I don't see — "

"Just curiosity," Lash said.

"It's Benton," she said, "Nell Benton."

Lash was not too surprised. "The ex-Mrs. Charles Benton?"

She nodded. "Now, will you let me alone?"

Lash shrugged. "Business isn't so good, Mrs. Benton. I find that I'll be able to handle your case, after all."

"I've changed my mind," Nell Benton retorted.

"You've hired another detective?"

"No — I've decided to drop the matter."

"Sure?"

"Quite sure."

"Because your ex-husband called on me?"

She looked at him steadily. "That has

nothing to do with it. I've just decided not to go ahead with the matter. That's final."

"All right, Mrs. Benton." He made a slight gesture over his shoulder. "How come you're living in a dump like this?" Her nostrils flared in annoyance and he went on, maliciously: "Isn't Charlie paying his alimony?"

"Get out of here!" she cried.

He grinned and walked past her, down the stairs to the walk. At the sidewalk he looked back and saw her, still standing in the doorway, looking at him. He waved to her and continued back to Hollywood Boulevard. There he crossed the street and waited for a bus to take him back to his apartment.

But as the bus pulled up to the curb he suddenly changed his mind and started walking down Hollywood Boulevard. He crossed Highland Avenue, went another block or two, then turned in at Eisenschiml's bookshop.

The old book dealer was fussing around with a first edition, repairing the binding. He grunted when he saw Lash. "What's all this about, Lash — this Alger stuff?"

"Nothing important, Oscar."

"No? Three days ago I sell an Alger book, then you come around. Then the customer comes around and says he didn't get his Alger book — that somebody using his name got it and then on top of that, a girl comes in here and wants to buy the same book. And you say it's nothing important . . . "

"Sterling Knox was here today?"

"Within the last hour and the girl only fifteen-twenty minutes ago. What's it all about, Simon?"

Lash said: "You made a nice profit on the book, didn't you?"

Eisenschiml grimaced. "I made a mistake; I thought it was eight-fifty I paid, instead of three-fifty."

"And your book scout paid ninety-five cents for it."

Eisenschiml scowled. "Are *you* charging by the hour, Simon?"

"I see what you mean. Soak the customer whatever he'll stand. This girl, who was just here — she was about twenty-two or twenty-three — a blonde?"

"About twenty-two or twenty-three

maybe, but she wasn't a blonde. A brunette."

"You're sure — I mean, that she was a brunette?"

"Sure, I'm sure. She wants me to get her a copy of *Ralph Raymond's Heir*."

"She left her name and address?"

Eisenschiml searched his desk for a moment, then picked up a card. "Clare — C–l–a–r–e, Halpin, Santa Ana Apartments, North Whitley — "

"Let me see that!" Lash snatched the card from Eisenschiml's hand. But the name and address merely verified Eisenschiml's reading of them.

Eisenschiml looked at him curiously. "You seem kinda surprised."

"I was expecting a different name and address."

"And a blonde?"

Lash frowned. "This business is beginning to get screwier right along."

"Oh, you'll make out on it all right," Eisenschiml said cheerfully. "And you'll get a nice, fat fee. Which reminds me, I just got in a beautiful copy of *Clay Allison of the Washita* . . . "

"I've got it."

"I know, but the copy you've got isn't a very good one. Look at this . . ." Eisenschiml pulled out a drawer and brought forth a paper-bound pamphlet. "This is a virtual mint copy, Simon. I never saw *Clay Allison* in as good shape as this."

Lash hesitated and was lost. "How much?"

"Well, you paid sixty-five dollars for that *poor* copy, Simon, and this is about as good a copy as you'll ever find. One of the rarest western Americana items . . ."

"How much?"

"A hundred and fifty, Simon . . ."

Lash glowered at the book dealer. "And you probably got it for three dollars . . ."

Eisenschiml exclaimed. "Are you trying to be funny? You never stumble on *this* book. I paid a Kansas City dealer one hundred and forty dollars for it. I really ought to have more, but — "

"All right," snapped Lash. "Put it on my account."

Eisenschiml wrapped up the book and Lash started to take his departure. But at the door, he stopped. "If anybody else comes in here asking about Alger, call me, will you, Oscar?"

"Sure thing, Simon."

Lash left the store and crossing the street, walked to Whitley, only a short distance away. He turned right and a half block away saw the Santa Ana Apartments, a modern ten-story building. He entered the lobby and approached the desk.

"Miss Halpin," he said to the clerk.

The clerk shook his head. "Sorry, she isn't in just now."

"How about Mr. Halpin?"

"He's out, too. Just went out again a few minutes ago. Do you care to leave a message?"

"No, it's all right."

Lash left the apartment house and continuing on to Sunset Boulevard, stepped aboard a westbound bus.

Entering his apartment, Lash heard Eddie Slocum out in the kitchen.

"Eddie," he called.

Eddie came out of the kitchen, only it wasn't Eddie. It was someone who had a handkerchief tied over his face — and a revolver in his hand.

Lash whirled to head for his desk, where reposed his own revolver. He didn't make it, for even as his hand closed on the drawer, lightning struck the back of his head. And that was all that he knew for some time.

9

WHEN he regained consciousness, Lash was lying on the red leather couch and Eddie Slocum was holding the kitchen ammonia bottle under his nostrils.

Lash pushed the bottle aside. "Take that damn thing away."

He sat up and pain shot through his head but he persevered and after a moment the pain became merely a dull throbbing.

"Who did it?" Eddie Slocum asked.

"Somebody with a handkerchief over his face. He was out in the kitchen when I came in. I thought it was you."

"Uh-uh, I found you on the floor when I came in, four-five minutes ago."

"What's missing?" Lash asked.

"Nothing that I can see, although I haven't had a chance to really look."

Lash got to his feet, discovered that he was as weak as a Persian kitten. But he made it to the desk.

"I thought so," he said. "The Alger book's gone."

"What the hell!" exclaimed Eddie Slocum. "This Alger business is working into a case. First thing you know somebody's going to get hurt."

"I've already been hurt," Lash said, "and if I find out who hit me on the head, somebody else is going to get hurt."

"Which reminds me," Eddie Slocum said, "I followed Oliver Halpin."

"To the Santa Ana Apartments?"

"Yeah, that's right. How did . . . well, that wasn't what I was really going to tell you. I followed Halpin — but somebody followed *me* . . . *!*"

"What?"

"And that ain't all, if you want to see the guy, just take a gander out of the front window. He followed me back. I thought I'd leave him out there for you to see."

Lash strode from the library, into the front bedroom. Peering through the Venetian blinds, he saw a '41 Ford coupe parked across the street.

He went back to the library and headed

for the stairs. "Want me?" Eddie asked.

"No, stay here."

Lash descended to the first floor, opened the door and started across the sidewalk and the street. A swarthy, shifty-eyed man with long sideburns, who lounged in the car, watched him curiously as he came up.

"All right," Lash snapped, "let's have it."

"Have what?" the swarthy man asked.

"You're casing my place," Lash said, "and you followed my assistant awhile ago."

"Did I?"

"You're a private eye."

"Am I?"

Lash scowled. "You work for some agency."

"Do I?"

"You don't look smart enough to work for yourself."

"Don't I?"

Lash tore open the car door and started to reach into the car for the swarthy one, but the latter took his right hand out of his coat pocket and showed Lash a snub-nosed revolver.

"What's this?" he asked pleasantly.

Lash let the car door swing shut. "My assistant is watching from the window," he said, "and he's already got your license number."

"Has he?"

Lash decided to change his tactics. "You're getting ten bucks a day — when you work. I've got twenty dollars here — "

"Have you?"

"Yes," snarled Lash, "I've got twenty dollars that says you don't know any other words than have you, and do you, and am I."

"Don't I?" asked the man in the car.

Lash gave it up and returned to the apartment to find Eddie Slocum just hanging up the telephone receiver. "I just called the license bureau — I've got a friend there. The car's registered under the name of Harry Cross . . . "

"Harry Cross, the double-crosser," Lash exclaimed.

He crossed to the desk and scooped up the loose-leaf address book. He found Harry Cross's number and dialed it. "Cross Protective Bureau," a feminine voice greeted him sweetly.

"Cross Protective Bureau!" Lash snorted. "Give me Harry Cross."

"Who shall I say is calling?" the operator asked sweetly.

"Simon Lash."

"One *mo*-ment, please!"

Harry Cross came on, in due time. "Simon," he said, enthusiastically. "How *are* you?"

"Listen, you chiseling double-crosser," Lash began and was interrupted.

"The same to you, sweetheart," Cross said smoothly.

"What's the idea of putting a tail on me?" Lash demanded angrily.

"Have I got a tail on you?"

"A stupid oaf, who thinks he looks like Rudolph Valentino. He's sitting outside my apartment right now."

"Is he?"

Lash exploded. "Now don't *you* give me that is he, do I, have I, routine!"

"I don't know what you're talking about, Simon," Harry Cross said, his tone as sweet as at the beginning of the conversation.

"I want to know who hired you to shadow me?" Lash snarled.

"Oh, is that so? Well, look, Simon, how much money have you got in the bank? Did your father beat your mother? And if you answer those questions I got some more for you. And when I run out of questions, maybe I'll tell you some of my private business. And then again, maybe I won't. How do you like that, sweetheart?"

Lash banged the receiver back on the hook.

Eddie Slocum whistled tunelessly and. Lash whirled on him.

"One more chirp out of you . . . !"

Eddie wisely headed for the kitchen and began banging pots and pans around. Lash went into the bedroom again and looked out. The Cross operator seemed to be taking a nap in his car.

He was about to turn away from the window, when the man in the car suddenly sat up and, leaning forward, apparently switched on the ignition. The coupe began to vibrate and then it shot away from the curb.

A black and white car rolled into the scene, swung to the curb in front of Lash's apartment. He turned away from the window and re-entered the library.

"Company, Eddie," he announced. "Cops."

"Oh-oh!" exclaimed Eddie.

The door buzzer whirred. Eddie looked inquiringly at Lash and the latter nodded.

Eddie went down the stairs and opened the door. A moment later he returned with a dyspeptic-looking, heavy-set man of about forty.

"Lieutenant Bailey!" exclaimed Lash.

"Hello, Lash," Lieutenant Bailey said sourly. "So you're in it again."

"In what?"

Bailey grunted. "I'm not in the pickpocket squad, you know."

"Oh, aren't you? There was a rumor that you'd be transferred out to East Los Angeles."

"Always the card, aren't you? Well, get your hat."

"I don't wear a hat in the house," Lash retorted.

"You're coming with me."

Lash shook his head. "I wish I could, Lieutenant, but I haven't finished the crossword puzzle in last Sunday's *Times*. It's a honey, too."

Bailey took a small slip of paper from his pocket — a piece about two inches by three, which had apparently been torn off a pad. "This is your name and address on here, isn't it?"

"Sure enough," Lash replied. "But the handwriting isn't very good."

"A man named Sterling Knox wrote it," Bailey said. "He wrote it on his telephone pad at the Lincoln Hotel . . . just before somebody put a bullet through him."

"Not me," Lash declared instantly.

"I didn't say you did it," Bailey exclaimed irascibly. "I said we want you to come down and answer some questions."

"I can answer all your questions with one word — no."

"You mean you won't talk?"

"I mean, I don't know anything to talk about."

"You're not working for Sterling Knox?"

"No."

"He didn't call you?"

"No."

"And you didn't call him?"

"No."

Bailey's face twitched angrily. "You mean to tell me you never even saw or heard of this Sterling Knox?"

"I didn't say that. I said that I wasn't working for him."

"Then you *do* know him?"

"I met him once."

"Then, get your hat and come with me."

Lash sighed wearily. "Here we go again!"

"You refuse to come with me?"

"If you haven't got a warrant — yes."

"What the hell do I want a warrant for?" Bailey cried. "I'm not arresting you. I just want you to come down to the station and answer some questions."

"I told you before that I wasn't employed by Sterling Knox. I met the man only once, for five minutes. I don't know who killed him or why. I don't know why he wrote my name and address on that piece of paper. There isn't one goddamn thing I can tell you about him. All I can say is no, no, no. And I can say that just as well here as down at your office. I can say it to you, to the chief of police and to the district

101

attorney. No, no, no!"

Bailey regarded Lash bitterly. "You're a private detective, Lash, you can talk like that to people. I can't. I'm a cop — and I've got people over me who can fire me."

"That's your hard luck," Lash said caustically.

"One of these days you're going to be out on a limb and somebody you talked to like that could help you, but he's going to remember things." The lieutenant shook his head and added, wistfully, "This might be the time."

"If it is, I'll get off the limb myself," Lash said, coldly.

"All right. Play it like that," Bailey said and took his leave.

When he was gone, Lash walked into the bedroom and stood at the window until the police car down below pulled away. And just as it did the Cross operator's coupe rolled quietly to the opposite curb and parked there.

Lash went back to the library. Eddie said: "So we're in it again."

"I've been expecting something like this," Lash replied. "Only I rather thought it would be the other one — Halpin." He nodded to the door. "Go out and take the Cross man with you. I want to go down to the Lincoln Hotel but I don't want him following me."

Eddie got his hat and took his departure. Lash, going into the bedroom, watched for the man across the street to follow Eddie Slocum. But he didn't. Lash could see Eddie down at the next corner and the man across the street still remained in his car.

Lash swore angrily and left the apartment. There was no need to look over his shoulder as he walked up the street. The coupe was following him in low gear. On Sunset Boulevard he got aboard a bus and the coupe followed him.

The private operator was fortunate, too, in finding a parking spot near the Lincoln Hotel.

10

LASH entered the hotel and saw the bell captain at his high stand. The man reacted violently when he saw Lash. He signaled to the basement stairs and Lash descended to the lower floor.

He went into the washroom, which was vacant, and a moment later the bell captain entered. His face was taut and he seemed very nervous.

"Jeez!" exclaimed the bell captain. "You shouldn't a come."

"Why not?"

"Ain't you heard what's happened?"

Lash nodded. "The man in Room eleven hundred and five . . ."

"Yeah and the place is swarming with cops. They been questioning everybody in the joint. Me, too."

"What'd you tell them?"

"What could I? I don't know anything."

"Did you tell them about me?"

The bell captain exclaimed, "You think I'm crazy! This Knox bird is just one of five hundred people in the hotel. I don't know him, I don't know anything about him."

"You're just as well off to stick to that story. But what *do* you know about him?"

"I just told you — nothing!"

"The police are still up in his room?"

"No, they took the body out a little while ago. They took a lot of pictures and some guy dusted the place for fingerprints, but I don't think they got anything. You can find too many different fingerprints in a hotel room."

"They sealed the room?"

"No, but they left orders not to rent it until they gave the okay."

"Good," said Lash, "now how about getting the key to the room?"

The bell captain recoiled as violently as if Lash had hit him in the face with his fist. "Gawd!" he cried. "Are you crazy?"

"I just want to look at the room a few minutes."

A shudder ran through the bell captain. "Uh-*uh!* Not me — I won't have anything to do with anything like that."

Lash took money out of his pocket; he

separated a twenty-dollar bill from the roll and held it out to the bell captain. The man shook his head, but it wasn't too quick a shake. Lash added another twenty-dollar bill and the bell captain groaned.

He took a passkey from his pocket. "This is just a passkey," he said. "It ain't got the hotel's name on it. You couldda found the key somewhere. I don't know anything about it."

"I could buy a key like that for fifty cents," Lash said. "For forty dollars I could buy eighty of them."

"What do you *want* me to do? Jump out of an eleventh floor window?" He looked down at the two twenties. "All right, Knox's place was a suite — a bedroom, sitting room and kitchen. From the bedroom there's an adjoining door to Suite eleven hundred and seven, see. The people in eleven hundred and seven checked out last night and it ain't been rented yet. This key'll let you into eleven hundred and seven —"

"And the latch is probably turned on the inside of eleven hundred and five," Lash said.

106

"I never thought of that. Yeah." The bell captain drew a deep breath. "All right, I'll do that. I'll go into eleven hundred and five and turn the bolt. Wait fifteen minutes, then go up to eleven hundred and seven, but look — if you're smart you'll ride to the tenth floor and walk up from there."

"I do those things right along." Then as the bell captain looked at him questioningly, he said, "What do you think I am — a second-story man?"

"How should I know?"

"You mean you'd take money even from a burglar?"

The bell captain scowled. "I don't know anything about anything."

"All right," said Lash. "I'm a private investigator."

"A private dick?" The bell captain relaxed.

"Make you feel better?"

The bell captain whistled softly. "How was I to know?"

He left the washroom. Lash waited a moment, then came out and went into the barbershop where he had another shoe shine. That job finished he ascended to the lobby and strolled to the elevators. He entered one and after a moment the car began to climb.

"Nine," Lash said.

He got out on the ninth floor and walked up to the eleventh. The corridor was deserted and Lash went directly to the door of Room 1107, unlocked it with his latchkey and entered. Inside, he locked the door with the key and then passing through into the bedroom paused before the door that led to Apartment 1105. He put his ear against the door and listened. He heard nothing.

Finally he inserted his key into the lock and turning it, opened the door. He stepped through and closed the door, but did not lock it. A hasty retreat might be necessary.

The room he was in was the bedroom of the suite. The bed was made up, but mussed. Policemen pawing it, no doubt. In the clothes closet hung several suits of clothes, a dressing gown and bathrobe. A half dozen pairs of shoes stood on the floor. The closet also contained four rather battered suitcases and a small steamer trunk.

Lash lifted the suitcases carefully. They were all empty. He tried the steamer trunk but found it locked. However, he raised one end and shook it lightly. As nearly as he could determine, it, too, was empty. Leaving the closet he surveyed the bedroom. It contained a chest of drawers and a dresser with a mirror. Lash started for the dresser, then decided to pass it up for the moment and went into the sitting room of the suite, where he had visited with Sterling Knox.

There was a dark, moist spot on the rug near the sofa, but otherwise there were no signs of the recent tragedy.

The only personal property of Sterling Knox was the bookcase with the Alger books.

Lash crossed to the case and looked at the books. He read a few of the titles: *Strong and Steady, Strive and Succeed, Ben the Luggage Boy, Young Bank Messenger, Walter Sherwood's Probation* and — *Ralph Raymond's Heir.*

Exclaiming under his breath, Lash tore the last book from the case. He whipped open the front cover. There was no inscription in the book.

He turned a couple of pages. It was a first edition all right and its state of wear was about the same as the copy of the book that Halpin had brought to Lash. But it wasn't the same book.

Lash riffled pages. There were no pencil marks, no underlined words in this book. It was merely a secondhand book with no identifying marks. There could be hundreds in existence just like it.

He counted the books in the bookcase. There were fifty-four. On a sudden impulse he went to the desk in a corner of the room and got a sheet of hotel paper. Fishing a pencil from his pocket he returned to the bookcase and began jotting down the titles of the books, abbreviating them. He was about halfway through when he heard a muffled phone ring. Startled, he went through into the bedroom, to the adjoining door that separated 1105 from 1107.

Yes, it was the phone in 1107. For a moment he was tempted to enter 1107 and answer the phone. It might be the bell captain calling him about something — warning him, perhaps. But Lash couldn't take the chance. 1107 was supposed to be unoccupied. It might be the desk — the housekeeper; someone who knew the suite was unoccupied.

As a precautionary measure, he put his key into the lock and turned it. He left it there. It would take but a second to turn the key to unlock the door.

He returned to the sitting room and examined the front door, leading to the corridor. It was locked. Nobody could surprise him from this side and he could retreat through the bedroom, into 1107 should anyone start unlocking the door.

He returned to the bookcase and continued jotting down the titles. He had only two or three books to go, when he thought he heard muffled voices. He strode quickly into the bedroom.

There were voices in 1107.

He put his ear to the door. A voice said: "It's one of our nicest suites, sir."

There was a muffled reply, then the first voice said more clearly: "The connecting door is locked."

Immediately, the doorknob was tried. Lash left the door and returned to the other room. His retreat was now cut off and he had to work fast.

He finished copying the Alger titles, then headed for the bedroom. But as he passed through the doorway, a feeling of premonition swept over him. He turned and went back into the living room. He went to the bookcase, took out the copy of *Ralph Raymond's Heir*, then he stepped out the hall door. He heard no sound but out in the corridor and, taking out his passkey, unlocked the door. He stepped out into the hall, put the key into the lock and was turning it as the elevator door nearby began to squeak. Lash jerked out the key as the elevator door opened.

"Down!" Lash called.

A man with a carnation in his buttonhole stepped out of the elevator. He looked sharply at Lash, turning away from the door of Room 1105.

"I beg your pardon," he began, but Lash brushed past him into the elevator.

He rode down to the first floor.

Passing through the lobby, he saw the bell captain staring at him. Lash nodded almost imperceptibly and continued on out of the hotel.

On the sidewalk, he shot a look down

the street to where the Cross operator was parked. The car came out from the curb. Lash, pretending to ignore it, strolled slowly down Hollywood Boulevard to Highland Avenue. The coupe had a difficult time moving so slowly.

He crossed Highland and proceeding a short distance, entered a bookstore. Inside, a clerk came forward, but Lash, shaking his head, strode through the store and left by the alley door.

In the alley he hurried back to Highland Avenue, turned right and, walking swiftly to the corner, crossed the street. A bus was just taking on passengers. Lash entered it and looking through the window saw the Cross coupe double-parked outside of the bookstore.

Fifteen minutes later he let himself into the apartment on Harper Street.

Eddie Slocum jumped up from the swivel chair behind the desk.

"There was a long distance call for you, from Mt. Miller, Illinois . . . "

"How long ago?"

"Not more than five minutes ago. You're to call Operator Fifty."

Lash picked up the phone, dialed

110 and said: "This is Simon Lash, at Granite two, one-one-two-seven. I understand you have a long distance call for me, from Mt. Miller, Illinois."

"Just a moment, please," said the operator. Then, "Oh yes, I'll see if I can get your party . . ."

Lash covered the mouthpiece with his hand and said to Eddie Slocum: "Anything else happen?"

"Halpin telephoned. But he wouldn't leave his number. Said he'd call in an hour . . . Did you lose the tail?"

"He lost me. Unless he got a ticket for double parking he's still waiting for me outside the Hollywood Bookstore."

The long distance operator said: "I have Mt. Miller for you. Here's your party, Mt. Miller."

Sam Carter came on the line. "Simon, I'm here in Mt. Miller and I've already got something for you."

"What?"

"Claude Benton — he's the local boy who went east and made good. You know who he is?"

"He owns Benton's Department Store in New York."

"You already knew!" Carter exclaimed.

"I didn't send you to Mt. Miller to learn that," Lash snapped. "I want to know what he did as a boy . . . "

"Well, holy cow, I've only been in town an hour. I thought you'd want to know about Benton. But I got some other things, too. This Oliver Halpin, he's a big shot, too. He had a dried milk business — a big outfit that he sold to Midwest Consolidated Dairies only a year or two ago. Got three million bucks."

"Now, I've got some news for you, Sam," Lash interrupted. "Give it out to the local paper and see what it stirs up. Sterling Knox was murdered here in Hollywood today . . . "

Carter inhaled sharply. "Holy cow! Say — are you mixed in it?"

"Of course not. But don't ask questions — I'm paying for this call. What else have you got?"

"Halpin — he's got a brother still living here. George Halpin lives on a farm and hates his brother's guts."

"Why?"

"He didn't say why."

"Well, find out why."

115

"Also, Simon, they had a telephone company here in eighteen ninety-seven — three hundred subscribers. I got a list of them. There was a man named Stuart Billings had a phone, but I haven't been able to locate him yet."

"If he had a phone fifty years ago he'd be at least eighty-five years old today and maybe as much as a hundred and twenty-five," Lash growled. "Find his descendants. And what about Clarissa?"

"No Clarissa. But there ain't no women subscribers in this phone book. The man was the boss of the family back in eighteen ninety-seven, you know. Which was a damn good thing, if you ask me. The biggest mistake this country ever made was to give women the vote — "

"Goddamn it, Sam," Lash snarled, "write me a letter — but don't waste my money telling me about it long distance. What else have you got . . . ?"

"Nothing, Simon, but you don't have to be so sarcastic . . ."

"Call me again when you get something."

"All right, Simon, but look — that hundred dollars . . ."

"I'm wiring it to you. Good-bye."

He slammed the receiver back on the hook and took out his billfold.

He skimmed out a hundred dollar bill, then got a five-spot from his trousers. "Here, Eddie, you'd better go down to Western Union and wire a hundred dollars to Sam Carter, Mt. Miller, Illinois . . . "

"He's working for us?"

"I'm paying him, but what work he's done so far you can stick in your ear."

As Eddie Slocum left the apartment Lash got the phone directory and looked up the number of the Santa Ana Apartments.

"Mr. Halpin's apartment," he said. Then a moment later when Halpin's voice said hello: "Mr. Halpin, this is Simon Lash . . . "

Halpin gasped. "How'd you know my number?"

"Are *you* kidding?"

Halpin said nervously: "I'll call you back."

"No, you won't," Lash cried. "I want to talk to you now. About Sterling Knox — "

"I said I'd call you back — in five minutes."

Lash got it, then. Halpin had someone in the room with him, someone he didn't want listening in on the conversation. His daughter.

"All right," Lash said. "I'll be waiting for your call. The number is Granite two, one-one-two-seven . . . "

11

HE hung up and waited a full two minutes by his watch. Then he dialed the Santa Ana Apartments and once more asked for Halpin's room. A woman's voice answered.

Lash said: "Miss Halpin, I understand you're looking for a copy of *Ralph Raymond's Heir*, by Horatio Alger, Jr."

"Is this Eisenschiml's bookstore?"

"No, it isn't, but I have a copy of the book. The point is, are you interested?"

There was a short pause. Then: "Why, yes, I might be. Can you tell me something about the book? I mean, is it a first edition?"

"It's a first edition," Lash replied. "And it's in what you'd call very good to fine condition."

"Is it autographed?"

"Must it be?"

"No, I just thought I'd ask. But, tell me, is there any sort of inscription in it at all?"

"There is," Lash said, "but it wasn't written in by Alger, if that's what you mean."

"It isn't, but in those old books you often find inscriptions, written in by the donors . . ."

"Well, there's one in here," said Lash. "But it doesn't mean anything, since — "

"What does it say?"

"Just a moment." Lash waited a moment. "It says: 'To Stuart, on his eleventh birthday, from his Aunt Clarissa.' And then the date, February second, eighteen ninety-seven . . ."

The girl's voice said, tautly: "I'd like to come over and get the book — where is your store?"

"I don't have a store," Lash said. "My business is in my home . . . I could send the book to you . . ."

"No, I'd like to get it tonight."

"Very well, then suppose you come over to my place." Lash gave her the address and hung up. Within ten seconds the phone rang.

"Mr. Lash," the voice of Oliver Halpin said, "I had a visitor at my apartment and I couldn't talk before."

"I gathered that. Look — you've heard about Sterling Knox?"

"What about him?" Halpin said, cautiously.

"He's dead. You haven't heard . . . ?"

Halpin hesitated. Then he said: "As a matter of fact, I just heard it over the radio a few minutes ago. Horrible."

"I think you'd better come over and talk to me," Lash said.

"What's there to talk about?"

"Sterling Knox."

"What've I got to do with Knox?" Halpin exclaimed. "I haven't seen the man in thirty years. I'm sorry about his death and all that, but I don't know a thing about it and — "

"I still think you'd better come over."

"I can't. And look, don't call me again at my apartment."

Lash suddenly snarled: "Now, *you* look, Halpin. You be at my apartment in an hour or there'll be police coming over to see you. Understand that?"

There was silence for a moment. Then Halpin said: "All right, I'll be there in an hour."

Lash hung up. Then he drew forward

the copy of *Ralph Raymond's Heir* and dipping a pen in an inkwell, wrote on the page facing the front cover: '*To Stuart, on his eleventh birthday, from his Aunt Clarissa, Feb. 2, 1897.*' He wrote in a cramped backhand that was supposed to be an imitation of a feminine style.

He blotted the inscription and closed the book.

Fifteen minutes later the door buzzer whirred. Simon Lash descended the stairs to the first floor and unlatched the door.

Clare Halpin was in her early twenties, a dark-haired slender girl. Very attractive, even more so than the former Mrs. Charles Benton.

She looked inquiringly at Lash: "Mr. Lash?"

"Yes. Will you come in?"

There was a little frown on her face. Although Lash had told her his business was in his home, she had apparently assumed that it would be a more public place than an upstairs apartment, on a side street.

Yet she entered and followed Lash up the stairs, into the library. When she saw the shelves of books she was reassured.

Lash went to one of the bookshelves and began scanning the books. "Rather odd, your wanting a Horatio Alger first edition," he said, over his shoulder.

"Why is it odd?"

"You don't find many women interested in first editions. Are you a collector?"

There was a slight pause. Then, "Yes."

"You've got quite a few Alger books, Miss Halpin?"

She made no reply and Lash moved to another shelf, still pretending to search for the Alger book.

Clare Halpin said: "The book's on your desk!"

"Oh, is it? I thought I saw it on one of these shelves."

He turned just as Clare Halpin picked up the book. She opened it and looked at the inscription. "How much is it?"

"Alger's getting pretty rare these days . . ."

" . . . How much?"

"As a matter of fact," said Lash, "I have another customer for that book and I really ought to give him a chance to make me an offer."

"Then why did you call me?" Clare Halpin asked sharply.

Lash smiled pleasantly. "In the book business — "

"*I* didn't come to you for this book," Clare Halpin interrupted. "*You* solicited me."

"That's right, I did. Well, shall we say — a hundred dollars?"

"A hundred dollars!" cried Clare Halpin. "What do you take me for?"

"You think the price is too high?"

"It's ridiculous. No Alger book is worth anything near that."

"Oh, no? How about *Now or Never?*"

"I have a copy of *Now or Never* that I got for ten dollars."

Lash said evenly: "Horatio Alger didn't write a book called *Now or Never.*"

Clare Halpin winced a little, but recovered quickly. "I must have confused it with an Alger title. They're so similar . . . I can't pay a hundred dollars for this — this book."

"I'll give it to you for nothing," Lash said, "if you'll tell me why you *really* want it?"

"I've told you . . . " Then she caught

124

herself. "What do you mean, you'll give it to me for nothing?"

"Just that. You're no collector of Alger. But your father is . . . "

"What do you know about my father?"

And at that very moment the door buzzer whirred. "What do I know about your father?" Lash asked grimly. "That's him, right now."

She inhaled sharply. "My father! Why should he — "

"I asked him to come here. But he wasn't due for another half hour . . . "

He started for the door, but Clare Halpin took a quick step after him. "Wait . . . ! Mr. Lash, Dad mustn't find me here."

"There's only the one door. He can't help but see you, if you leave."

Her eyes darted wildly to the kitchen door. "Couldn't I go in there?"

"You're not going to like what you hear."

"That can't be helped. But Father mustn't see me. That's — that's important . . . Please . . . !"

"All right," Lash said, "go in there. And keep quiet."

He opened the door to the stairs as she headed for the kitchen. He went down and unlatched the front door. Oliver Halpin pushed in.

"Now, what's this all about?" he demanded angrily.

"You're early . . ."

"What of it?" snapped Halpin. He followed Lash up the stairs. In the library he said: "Of course you know I'm going to fire you, after this."

"I've already fired *you*," Lash said evenly. "And whether I send the police after you depends entirely on you."

"I'm not afraid of the police."

"Then why are you here?"

"Because I want to know what your game is. I hired you on a confidential matter yesterday — "

"Oh, was it confidential?"

Halpin gritted his teeth. "So you *are* that sort! All right, keep the five hundred I gave you. I'll charge it up to experience. But we're through."

"Good!" snapped Lash. "We're through. But I don't think the police are through. They're still looking for the person who killed Sterling Knox."

Halpin looked at Lash for a long moment. Then he crossed to a chair and seated himself. "How much?" he asked.

Lash's eyes narrowed. "How much, what?"

"You're blackmailing me, aren't you? I asked, how much?"

Lash said: "I could pick you up and throw you down the stairs!"

"You probably could. But you'd rather have the money. Well, I said I was willing to pay."

"You haven't got enough money."

"Oh yes, I have. I've got a lot of money."

"The three million you got from the Midwest Consolidated Dairies?"

"So you know about that."

"I know quite a lot about you."

"It seems that you do. I guess that's the way you fellows work."

"Look," said Lash, "I'm going to disappoint you terribly. I'm not going to blackmail you. I'm not going to make you cough up a red penny. In fact, I'm going to give you back your five hundred dollars and forget that I ever saw you.

That is — if you answer just two little questions."

Halpin studied Lash with his head cocked to one side. "What are the questions?"

"One: who is Stuart, who was eleven years old on February second, eighteen ninety-seven?"

Halpin drew a deep breath. "That's what I was paying *you* money to find out."

"I don't believe that."

"But it's true."

"Let's leave it for a moment. The other question: Why do you want to know who this Stuart was? And I don't want the curiosity answer again."

Halpin sighed wearily. "I'm afraid you're going to have to go to the police."

"You won't answer that question?"

"The answer's the same as it always was — the one you won't believe."

"Halpin," said Lash, harshly. "A man's been murdered because of that question."

"You're crazy!" Halpin cried indignantly. "Sterling Knox's death had nothing to do with this."

"I think it has. And I also think I could add another murder to that . . . a boy named Stuart . . . "

Astonishment came slowly over Halpin's features. Then he got to his feet. "Now, I *know* you're crazy. Here — give me my book and let me out of here . . . "

12

HE headed for the book which was lying on Simon Lash's desk. Lash let him pick it up. Then Halpin flipped open the cover, closed it and flipped it open again. He looked at Lash.

"What kind of a game are you trying to pull?"

"Me?" asked Lash innocently.

"This isn't the book I gave you."

"The book you gave me was called *Ralph Raymond's Heir*, wasn't it?"

"Yes, but this inscription . . . "

"It's the same — 'To Stuart, on his eleventh birthday, from his Aunt Clarissa . . . '"

"It's a forgery," Halpin said thickly. "It isn't the book I gave you and I want — "

"What's the difference?" snapped Lash. "It's *Ralph Raymond's Heir* and it's a first edition, in as good condition as the other book. And the inscription's the

130

same. What's the difference if it wasn't written by the real Aunt Clarissa? She's dead by now, anyway."

By the time Lash finished Halpin was trembling violently. "It isn't the same and you know it."

"Was Aunt Clarissa a famous person? Is her autograph worth anything?"

"That's not the point. I gave you a certain book and I want *that* book back."

"All right, then all you have to do is find the man who stuck a gun in my face and" — Lash touched the back of his head — "knocked me on the head with the gun. He's got your book. If you won't want this one, put it down."

Halpin dropped the book on the desk. "I don't know what your game is, Lash — "

"Maybe I haven't got a game. Maybe I just don't like anyone to make a sucker of me."

"You mean I tried to — "

"Yes. You haven't told me one word of truth since you came to me."

"This is ridiculous, Lash," cried Halpin. "I employed you yesterday on a simple matter of tracing down the ownership of

131

a book. Today, you've got it all tied up with murder and robbery and slugging. Put yourself in my position . . . "

"No, thanks," Lash said.

"You say you're going to throw me to the police — why, if you're as honest as you pretend to be?"

"Because I — working for you — got involved in the death of Sterling Knox. The police were here once today. They'll be back. And they can make things tough for me. As a matter of fact, if they knew everything they'd *arrest* me. And in that case I'd have to tell them I was working for you."

"But working for me didn't entail going to Sterling Knox!" Halpin complained.

"Oh, no? You told me *you* were Sterling Knox. And when I found out that you weren't, I put my foot into it. There's a man at the Lincoln Hotel who can identify *you* as the man who impersonated Sterling Knox — at least to the extent of intercepting his mail. How do you think the police will regard that? And — come with me . . . " Lash started abruptly into the front bedroom. At the window he waited for Halpin, who came in laggingly. "Look across the street," Lash said, for the Cross operator had resumed his post. "That car's been there all day. Every time one of us leaves this place we're followed . . . "

"Police?" Halpin asked thickly.

"A private detective. I've checked on him — he works for the Cross Agency, a big outfit, with none too savory a reputation. Get *them* after you and you'll have something to worry about."

Halpin groaned. "But where's this all going to end?"

"I don't know. I do know it isn't going to end until the police have arrested the person who murdered Sterling Knox."

"Who — who do you think did it?"

"Maybe you," Lash said.

"No!"

"If you didn't do it, you've nothing to worry about. You may have some rough times, but in the end you'll come out all right. I promise you that. You could save yourself a lot of grief if you told me the truth."

"I can't tell you the truth, because I don't know it."

Lash led the way back into the library.

133

Halpin followed him and looked longingly at the door leading to the street stairs. "I'd tell you if I knew, Lash, but I don't know."

"You know who Stuart was?"

"I had a cousin named Stuart, when I was a boy in Mt. Miller," Halpin finally admitted. "The Stuart you're trying to trace down *may* have been my cousin. I don't know. The similarity of the names — Stuart and Aunt Clarissa, who was my mother, caught my eye. But thousands of Alger books were sold — millions, I've heard. Fifty Stuarts could have been given an Alger book by fifty Aunt Clarissas."

"But you don't believe that — in view of what I've told you. That this particular book was owned by Claude Benton, within five years after its original purchase."

"Well, I *think* this is the book my mother gave Stuart."

"It is — you can bet two of your three million dollars that it is. All right, what was your cousin Stuart's full name?"

Halpin hesitated. "Stuart Billings. His mother was my mother's sister."

"What happened to him?"

"He died when he was about fifteen or sixteen."

"What year?"

"I guess I was about fourteen."

"When he was sixteen, then?"

"That's right. He was a couple of years older than I was."

"What did he die of?"

"Pneumonia or something like that."

"What's something like pneumonia?"

"I don't remember what he died of — I was only a boy at the time."

The phone rang and at the same time Eddie Slocum pushed open the door and entered. He shot a quick glance at Lash, then at Oliver Halpin and headed for the kitchen.

Lash tried to give him a signal but it was too late. Eddie was already opening the kitchen door. The phone on Lash's desk kept ringing.

He picked it up. "Yes?"

The operator said: "Mt. Miller, Illinois, calling Simon Lash."

"Speaking."

Lash tried to keep his free ear tuned for noises in the kitchen, but then Sam

135

Carter came on the wire. "Simon, it's midnight here and this town's dead. I'm going to hit the hay myself, but I thought I'd give you a buzz and tell you that I've located this Stuart fellow — "

"So have I," Lash said.

"Then I'm wasting my time," Sam Carter retorted. "Anyway, if it's the same one I've located he's been dead forty-five years."

"Yes, I know. Look — I've got company at the moment. I'll call you back . . . "

"But I haven't got a phone in my room," Sam Carter howled. "I'm down in the lobby of the hotel and it'll mean hanging around here — "

"Well, hang around!" Lash snapped and slammed the receiver back on the hook.

He looked up and Eddie Slocum re-entered the room from the kitchen. He nodded casually to assure Lash that the situation was under control. "Feel like some coffee, boss?"

"Not now, Eddie. I'm going to bed in a little while."

Eddie went back into the kitchen and

136

Lash returned to Halpin. "Mr. Halpin," he said, "do you have a specimen of your mother's handwriting?"

Halpin grunted. "I know what you're getting at — the inscription in the book; you wonder why I didn't recognize it as my mother's handwriting. Well, she died forty years ago. The only handwriting of hers I've got is an entry in the family Bible. I compared it with the inscription in the book and I don't know. Penmanship has changed so much in forty years — it's individual today, but in the old days it all looked more stilted. I *think* the writing in the book was my mother's . . . "

"You could have paid a handwriting expert a lot less than five hundred dollars."

"I did just that, Lash. He said the handwriting seemed to be the same, but he ought to have more of a sample to make absolutely sure. I came to you to verify his findings."

Lash looked closely at Halpin for a moment, then spread out his hands. "All right, Mr. Halpin, do you want me to continue?"

"Are you going to tell the police?" Halpin countered.

"I'm not going to tell them anything I don't have to. But if it comes to a showdown, or if they hear of you through another source, I'm going to tell them the truth. I've *got* to. I have a detective agency license, you know, and the police can have it revoked if they can prove any act of illegality or law-breaking on my part."

"Yes, I understand that." Halpin went to the door and with his hand on it, hesitated. "I'd like you to continue, Mr. Lash — and I'd like to get that book back."

Lash nodded and Halpin went down the stairs. Lash waited until he heard the door open and close, then went to the kitchen.

"You can come out now," he said to Clare Halpin.

She was sitting on the kitchen stool, having a cup of coffee that Eddie Slocum had brewed. She set down the cup and followed Lash into the library.

"You heard?" he asked.

She nodded. "It was no worse than I'd

138

already suspected, but . . . " she paused. "I didn't know you were a detective."

"I never told you I was a bookseller."

"But how did you know I — I wanted to get that book?"

"You asked a book dealer to get it for you — Oscar Eisenschiml." He gestured to the walls. "Most of these books came from Eisenschiml at one time or another." He looked at her sharply. "Why *did* you want a copy of *Ralph Raymond's Heir* — when your father already had one?"

She hesitated. "During the past year Dad had six or seven copies of *Ralph Raymond's Heir*. He had a book dealer in Chicago advertising for one, and one in New York. They sent him a book every month or two and each time that it came Dad got excited about it, but the minute he unwrapped it he lost interest and threw the book away. Then a few days ago he got another and became even more excited than usual. And he remained excited for awhile. But then the book disappeared and he's been terribly depressed ever since. I didn't pay so much attention the other times but this time I decided to find out what there was in this book that always affected him so greatly."

Lash nodded thoughtfully. "Where were you born, Miss Halpin?"

"Chicago."

"Have you ever been in Mt. Miller?"

"Oh yes — many times. Although Dad moved his office to Chicago he went to the plant at Mt. Miller frequently and I sometimes went with him."

"Did you know Sterling Knox?"

"Why yes, I met him on those visits to Nell."

Lash almost held his breath for a moment. "Nell Knox?"

"I went to school with her."

Lash hesitated a moment. "You knew about her marriage."

"And her divorce."

"How long since you've seen her?"

"Not since she got married — almost two years ago."

"Her marriage didn't last very long."

"Six months, which is just six months longer than *I* would have remained married to that insufferable nincompoop."

"You don't like Charles Benton?"

Clare Halpin answered that with a grimace. Lash said, casually: "You haven't seen Nell then, since coming out here to Hollywood?"

"No." Then Clare's eyes widened. "You mean — she's *here* in Hollywood, right now?"

"Yes — and so is her ex-husband."

"You know where Nell is staying?" Clare asked eagerly.

"At the Oro Grande Apartments. That's on Orange Drive, right near the Lincoln Hotel."

"I'm going to look her up," Clare exclaimed.

"Now?"

"Nell won't mind."

She started for the door. Lash started to call her back, then changed his mind.

Eddie Slocum came out of the kitchen. "Nice girl," he observed.

Lash reached for the telephone and dialed Long Distance. "I want to get Sam Carter at Mt. Miller, Illinois," he told the operator. "He's staying at the hotel — whatever hotel there is in that town."

The call was put through promptly,

141

but Lash, not being cut off, heard the night clerk at the hotel say: "He ain't here right now. But he said if anybody called him Long Distance — "

The operator chose that moment to cut Lash off. Then a moment later she cut him in. "Sorry, your party cannot be reached just now. Shall we try later?"

"No," snapped Lash and hung up the receiver.

He got to his feet. "I'm hitting the hay Eddie."

Eddie yawned. "Shall I tell the guy in the Ford, across the street?"

"No, and I hope the fog rolls in and he gets pneumonia."

13

LASH was awakened the next morning by the jangling of the telephone in the library. But he let it jangle. Eddie Slocum would answer it. And he did, but he came into Lash's bedroom a moment later.

"Mt. Miller is calling you, Chief," he announced.

Lash groaned. "What time is it?"

"Ten minutes to six."

"Tell Sam I'll call him in an hour."

"It isn't Sam Carter on the phone," Eddie said. "It's the Sheriff of Miller County, Illinois."

Lash swung his feet to the floor and strode from the bedroom into the library. He crossed to the desk and grabbed up the phone. "Simon Lash talking!"

"This is Sheriff Walters," said a voice on the phone. "There's been an accident here in Mt. Miller — "

"A man named Sam Carter?" Lash asked quickly.

"Why, yes," was the reply. "There was a telegram in the man's pocket, where it says you sent him a hundred dollars and — "

"He's dead?"

"Well, yes," the sheriff admitted.

"You've got the person who killed him?"

"Well, no, you see it wasn't a person. It was a — well, a bull . . . "

"A bull!" exclaimed Lash.

"Well, yes. You see, he musta tried to cross this here pasture where the bull was — "

"Bull, my eye! Sam Carter was murdered. And not by a bull."

There was silence for a moment, then the sheriff said, mildly: "What makes you say that, Mr. Lash?"

"Because Sam Carter was a detective and he was in Mt. Miller working on a case — "

"What case?"

"The case of a man named Alger," Lash snapped.

"There ain't nobody livin' here by the name."

"That's right — Alger's dead. But

144

that's why Carter was there — to find out who killed him."

The sheriff's voice remained calm and unexcited. "Well now, I find that a little hard to believe."

"Then why did you telephone me?" Lash demanded angrily.

"Because there wasn't no identification on him except this-here telegram and we figured you might be his next of kin, sending him money like that. And there's the matter of the body."

"Call Chicago," Lash said. "Sam Carter was a private detective there and the police will know all about him. And a good morning to you, sir!"

Lash put the receiver back on the hook. For a moment he stared at it, then looked up at Eddie Slocum who was watching him from the other side of the room.

"Sam Carter got it?" Eddie asked.

Lash nodded. "And the rube sheriff insists a bull killed him." He exhaled heavily. "Call up the airport, Eddie — find out when the next plane leaves for Chicago."

"You're going to Mt. Miller?"

"Looks like I have to."

145

Lash went back into the bedroom and began dressing. He was packing a suitcase when Eddie entered. "If you skip breakfast you can just make the Chicago plane. I've ordered a taxi unless you want me to drive you to the airport."

"No. As soon as the stores open get down to a grocery and load up enough for two or three days. I want you to stay right here in the apartment all the time I'm gone — where I can reach you in a hurry if I want you."

A horn honked outside the apartment. Lash got his topcoat out of the closet and headed for the door. There was a dubious expression on Eddie Slocum's face as he watched Lash leave.

Down on the street, Lash got into the taxi. "Airport," he said. As the cab started off he looked through the rear vision window. The Ford was following. Lash smiled grimly.

14

SIMON LASH landed at the Chicago airport shortly before five o'clock — Central time. A half hour later a chartered plane, with Lash as the sole passenger, took off from the same airport and at precisely six-thirty Lash stepped to the ground of a reconverted cow pasture.

Carrying his topcoat and suitcase he walked toward a man who was tinkering on a jalopy.

"How do I get to Mt. Miller from this town?" he asked the mechanic.

"Bus," replied the mechanic. "Only it's left by now."

"How far is it to Mt. Miller?"

"'Bout six miles."

Lash took a ten-dollar bill from his pocket. "Does this crate run?"

The man took the ten-dollar bill and slammed down the hood of the car. "Let's try it out, huh?"

The car had a hopped-up motor. The

mechanic never let it out entirely but in five minutes after stepping into the car, Lash was in Mt. Miller. The driver of the car slowed down to fifty. "Any special place in town you want to go?"

"The hotel."

A moment later the car squealed to a stop in front of a dingy two-story building. "Hotel," the driver said.

Lash got out and waved to the driver of the hopped-up car. Then he entered the hotel.

The lobby was about twenty feet square and contained, besides a desk, three shabby leather-covered chairs, a leather-covered couch and about six big brass spittoons.

At one side of the desk was a wide door that led into a small dining room. There were six or eight diners in the room, but the lobby contained only two people, a middle-aged mustached man seated in one of the leather chairs reading a Chicago newspaper and the man behind the desk, a roly-poly, fat-jowled man with snaggled, stained teeth.

"Room and bath," Lash said.

"Room," replied the clerk, "but you

take your own bath!" He howled at his own joke.

"Funny," Lash said.

The clerk continued to chortle, but after awhile recovered enough to turn the hotel register about so Lash could sign it. "Room'll cost you four dollars — American plan, or two dollars European." He read Lash's signature. "Simon Lash, Hollywood, California. Well, well . . . !"

Behind Lash the middle-aged man lowered his newspaper and got to his feet. "You're Mr. Lash?" he called. "I talked to you on the telephone this morning."

"Sheriff Walters?"

The man nodded. "Musta flown here, huh?"

"That's right."

"Sorry about your friend, Carter," the sheriff said. "I talked to his wife on the phone this morning and she said to have the body shipped to Chicago. Got it out this afternoon."

"You've already shipped it."

"Yes."

"Without an autopsy?"

The sheriff grimaced. "Wasn't any

need for an autopsy. Like I told you, he was killed by a bull . . . "

"The bull confessed?"

The sheriff scowled. "Now, look here, Mr. Lash, that ain't no way to talk. I been sheriff of this county for twelve-thirteen years."

"How many murders have you had in that time?"

"People around here don't commit murders. Had a manslaughter case four-five years ago, but murder . . . " The sheriff shuddered.

Lash turned to the hotel clerk. "Can you tell me where George Halpin lives?"

Before the clerk could reply, the sheriff said: "It was George Halpin's bull killed your friend."

Lash whirled. "And you *still* say Sam Carter wasn't murdered?"

The sheriff stared at him. "Are you insin — insinuatin' that George Halpin . . . " He couldn't bring out the word, not in association with a man he knew so well.

Lash said to the clerk: "Will you look after my bag?" He indicated the bag on the floor and dropped his topcoat on it.

Then he headed for the street door.

Outside, Lash stood on the hotel doorstep and surveyed Mt. Miller. He could see most of it. He stood at the very edge of the business section. It ran four blocks from his vantage point and then the cornfields began. There were four cross streets, each of which ran for two or three blocks to the right and left of Main Street before they, too, petered out into farm fields.

Across the street and midway down the first block was a store with a neon sign over it: *Club Café*.

Lash crossed the street and walked toward the Club Café. As he came up he looked into the window and saw that it was, as he expected, the local gin mill. It contained a combination bar and soda fountain on one side of the room, three booths on the other and in the rear a small area, with two or three tables and enough space left over for whatever local jitterbugs felt in need of exercise.

Lash entered the café and sat down on a high stool. A man with pomaded hair and an Adolphe Menjou mustache — and there the similarity ended — slid over and polished the counter in front of Lash.

"Beer," Lash said.

The man got a bottle and opened it. As Lash poured beer into a glass he said, "Is there a taxicab in town?"

"Unh-uh."

"Anybody ever rent a car?"

"Unh-uh."

Lash took out money to pay for his beer. He searched through a thick roll, but found nothing smaller than a twenty. And there were quite a few larger bills in the roll, which the bartender couldn't help but see.

"Any place in town where a man can have some fun?" he asked.

"Unh-uh," said the man behind the counter. But his nostrils were flaring a little and he couldn't take his eyes off Lash's bankroll, which Lash still held in his fist.

"Anybody in this town ever been in jail?" Lash persisted.

The man behind the bar did not say 'Unh-uh,' this time. He moistened his lips with his tongue, turned to the cash register and scraped together practically all the money in the machine, to make change for the twenty-dollar bill.

He brought the money to Lash and counted it out. Lash said evenly: "Keep the change."

A little shiver ran through the bartender. He looked at the money and he looked at Lash. Then he leaned over the bar and resting his right hand on the wood, flicked his index finger over to the left.

"Him," he said.

There was a man at the far end of the bar. He had an empty beer glass in front of him and he sat on a high stool with both of his hands in his coat pockets. He was looking into the back-bar mirror with a vacant expression.

Lash said to the bartender, "Two more beers."

Then he got up from his stool and moved down to the stool next to the man who had once been in jail. The bartender brought the two bottles of beer, set them down in front of Lash. Lash moved one a few inches to his left.

"On me," he said.

For a long moment, the man who had once been in jail continued to stare into

153

the mirror. Then he sighed a little and, picking up the bottle of beer, poured some of the pale amber liquid into his glass. Still looking into the mirror, he said: "Thanks."

Lash drank some of his own beer, then said. "Lived around here long?"

"All my life, except a year," was the reply.

The man was about thirty, so he had lived in Mt. Miller about twenty-nine years.

"My name's Lash," said Lash, "Simon Lash."

"Clyde," said the other man. "Harry Clyde." His shoulders hunched up and he stared into the mirror again. "What's the game?"

"No game. I'm looking for a man who's got a car who can drive me about town. Someone who knows people around Mt. Miller."

Clyde took his left hand from his pocket and poured out some more beer. He drank it and set the glass down on the bar. Then he said: "There was a stranger in town yesterday. He went around, too, and he asked a lot of people a lot of questions. He got killed by a bull last night."

"He was working for me," Lash said.

"There are a lot of bulls on the farms around here," Clyde said. "But me, I never go into pastures."

"Have you got a car?"

"Kind of a car.

Lash took out his money again and skinned out a hundred-dollar bill. "There'll be another of these this time tomorrow if I still need you."

Clyde took the hundred-dollar bill and examined it. "That year I was telling you about, that I didn't live in Mt. Miller. I spent it in Joliet."

"Is that so?"

"A traveling salesman had me drive him around and he said I stuck him up."

"Did you?"

"Yes."

Lash got up from his stool. "Shall we go?"

Clyde got to his feet. "As long as you know." He followed Lash to the door. There was an old Model T at the curb. It had wheels, with some rubber on them and it probably had a motor somewhere under the rusted tin.

Clyde got in behind the wheel and did some things and the car began to make noise and vibrate. He looked at Lash who climbed in beside him. "George Halpin's place?" Clyde finally asked.

"You've got the idea."

Clyde backed away from the curb and started down the street. He drove to the far end of town, where a paved highway intersected Main Street. He turned left and headed toward the setting sun.

On the left was a series of long, low buildings. A sturdy, mesh-steel fence surrounded them and as they passed a gate, Lash noted the sign: Midwest Consolidated Dairy Products Company.

"Oliver Halpin's old place," he observed.

"Yeah," Clyde replied. "And that's George's place up there on the right." He suddenly began braking the old flivver and brought it to a stop, opposite a field. "The bull."

The field was about five acres and fenced with barbed wire. A red bull stood in the center of the field, looking at the car on the road.

"He's mean," Clyde remarked.

"All bulls are mean," Lash retorted.

"This one's smelled blood."

"You think he killed Sam Carter?"

"The point is, *you* don't think so."

"I don't."

"I saw the body. Albert mauled him all right."

"After he was dead?"

"The sheriff says before he was dead."

"You know what I think of your sheriff?"

"I can guess."

"Am I right?"

"No."

Clyde worked the pedals of the flivver and the machine shot forward. A quarter of a mile beyond the bull pasture he began slowing up. Then, as he came to a gate, he made a sharp right turn and coasted to a stop before a sprawling, unpainted frame house.

"Here we are!"

Lash got out of the car, but Clyde remained behind the wheel. As he started toward the house, a man came out, a man who bore a facial resemblance to Oliver Halpin. But he was several years younger and at least fifty pounds heavier. He was smoking a corncob pipe. He came down a short flight of stairs, looked at Lash and called to Clyde in the car.

"Hiya, Clyde."

Clyde waved a response. Then Halpin said to Lash: "Been expectin' you, Mr. Lash."

"The sheriff told you I was coming out?"

"Yeah, said you'd be out in a half hour. Didn't miss it much."

"Then you also know why I'm here?"

"'Bout Albert, isn't it?"

"Albert?"

Halpin waved in the general direction of the pasture. "My bull."

"A good bull, is he?"

"Took a blue ribbon at the State Fair, only two years ago."

"How many people has he killed so far?"

"Just one. And anybody who hasn't got more sense than to go crossing a bull pasture in the middle of the night deserves to get killed."

"You think Sam Carter *walked* into

that pasture last night?"

"How else would he get there?"

"How else would he?"

Halpin smiled blandly. "Look, Mr. Lash, the sheriff says Sam Carter was some kind of detective from Chicago and I hear you're a detective, too — "

"Only I'm from Hollywood — not Chicago."

"Walters says Carter was working for you. All right, Carter came around here last night, asking a lot of fool questions. Then he went away and this morning I found him out in the pasture. All right, I'm sorry, but he was trespassing on my property. Albert didn't follow him into town and kill him — he didn't even break out of the pasture. He was in his own place, his home, you might say. So what can you make of it?"

"Murder."

Halpin snorted. "You'll have yourself one sweet time makin' murder out of a bull killing a man in his own home."

"A man who used to live around here was murdered yesterday, out in California. A man named Sterling Knox. You've heard about it?"

Halpin hesitated. Then he nodded. "I've got a radio."

"You heard it on the radio? I thought Sam Carter might have told you — last night."

"He didn't mention it."

"I don't mean the first time he was out here, because he didn't know about it then. The second — "

"There wasn't any second trip. I mean, I talked to him only the one time."

"What did you talk about?"

"He asked me if I had a brother named Oliver and I told him yes."

"Where's your brother now?"

George Halpin scowled. "In California. Ain't you workin' for him?"

"Should I be?"

"Yes. Ollie and me ain't talked together for thirty years."

"Thirty years — or forty?"

"Since I was twenty-one years old — that's thirty years ago. More or less." Halpin jerked a thumb angrily toward the road. "Ollie sold that place up the road to Midwest Dairies for three million dollars. I got an eighty-acre farm here and a mortgage of eight thousand dollars.

160

You'd think Ollie'd be satisfied, wouldn't you?"

"Isn't he?"

"He won't be satisfied until I'm dead."

"That's a pretty harsh thing to say about a brother, Mr. Halpin."

"Is it? Well, what my brother did to me was pretty harsh, too. I just told you he's got three million dollars. By rights, half of that money should be mine."

"You owned a half interest in the dried milk plant?"

"I owned a half interest in the dairy, that Ollie started with. He squeezed me out of it."

"When was that?"

"I told you. That's why we stopped talking. Ollie no sooner got me out of the business, than he switched over from making butter to making dried milk and dried buttermilk. He had it in mind all the time; that's why he wanted me out of the business. He knew he'd make a million dollars."

"Three million."

"All right, three million."

"And you say he froze you out of the dairy?"

Halpin gestured over his shoulder at the house. "This was part of the dairy, then. He said I could have it and he'd take the dairy."

"How much was the dairy worth at the time?"

The question seemed to annoy Halpin. "That ain't the point. It was what he done with the dairy as soon as he got me out of it."

"You said this was an eighty-acre farm — was it stocked at the time you got it?"

"Of course, it was part of the dairy. Say — what're you trying to make out? That Ollie did fair by me?"

"I don't know. How much was the farm — and the stock — worth at the time?"

"We called it twenty thousand."

"And the dairy?"

"Twenty — " Then Halpin caught himself. "Now, look here, that's the same argument he's used all these years. I told you, it wasn't a matter of what the dairy was worth then — it was the scheme he had for changing over to the dried milk business. He didn't tell me at the time

162

we made the deal that he was going to do that."

"You know what I think?" Lash said. "I think you got a fair deal. You got a farm with a lot of livestock on it. Your brother took a country dairy and — "

"Get out of here!" Halpin said, thickly. "Get to hell off this place and don't come back."

Lash walked coolly back to the flivver and got in beside Harry Clyde. Clyde waved to George Halpin, started the flivver and made a sharp turn. He headed back for the road, but stopped before he turned on to the pavement.

"Now where?"

"Your local newspaper — do you know the publisher?"

"Chet Remington? Sure."

15

HE turned left on the pavement and headed back for Mt. Miller. At Main Street, he turned right and in the second block pulled up before a one-story building. Lettering on the window read: *Mt. Miller Gazette*. It was getting dark outside, but there was a light on in the building. Lash got out of the flivver and entered the newspaper office.

The office consisted of a small room, containing two desks and several chairs. An open door revealed a small print shop behind the office. A man who looked as if he had consumption sat at one of the desks, reading galley proofs.

He looked up as Simon Lash entered. "Mr. Lash, isn't it?"

"The sheriff works fast."

The newspaper publisher grunted. "How many strangers you think we get in this town every day? . . . Walters told me this morning that he talked to you long distance and you weren't in town five minutes before I knew all about you. And it wasn't the sheriff who told me, either."

"The hotel clerk?"

The newspaper man grunted. "Detective, aren't you? What're you trying to do — make murder out of what happened last night?"

"Any objections?"

The newspaper man suddenly got up and held out his hand. "My name's Chester Remington. What can I do for you?"

"You mean you don't care if I *do* find out that Sam Carter was murdered?"

"I'd love it. I could make two-three hundred dollars writing up the case for one of the true detective magazines, not to mention what the Chicago papers would pay me for sending them the stuff, at space rates." He rubbed his hands together. "Did you get anything from Sam Carter before he, uh, before he died?"

Lash shook his head. "You met Sam?"

"He was in here, looking over the old issues of the paper — from my father's time."

"Your father owned this paper before you?"

"He started it in eighteen eighty-eight."

"And you've got file copies of every issue from the beginning?"

"I sure have."

"I'd like to see them, beginning with eighteen ninety-seven."

"Carter stopped reading in nineteen hundred and two. It was then that he found what he wanted."

"How do you know?"

"I was here, wasn't I? He copied something out of a nineteen hundred and two paper, then he stopped reading."

"Let's have the nineteen hundred and two file, then."

Remington pointed to one of the other desks. "There it is. I hadn't put it away yet." He grimaced. "As a matter of fact, I was going through it myself just a few minutes ago. Thought maybe I might find the same thing Carter found."

"Did you?"

"I don't know. I wasn't paying too much attention to him last night and when he got through writing down whatever it was he found, he closed

166

the book. But as nearly as I could remember, he was reading about three-fourths of the way through the volume and . . . here . . . !"

Remington came around from his desk, went to the other desk and opened the bound file copy of the *Mt. Miller Gazette*. He turned pages and finally stopped at the September 24th issue. He stabbed at a front page story.

"It could be this."

Lash glanced at the item. The headline read: '*Pneumonia Takes Stuart Billings*.'

The account was an extensive one for a sixteen-year-old boy, who had died of apparently natural causes, but as Lash read he learned the reason for that. Stuart was the son of the late Ralph Billings and Ralph Billings, it seemed, was one of the founders of Mt. Miller, Illinois. He had been the town's leading merchant. He also owned the Mt. Miller bank and had been, up to the time of his untimely death two years previously, the leading citizen of the community.

In fact, the obituary was more of a eulogy for Ralph Billings than it was for young Stuart Billings, his son.

But it was in the last paragraph of the story that Lash found what he sought. It read: 'Burial will be from the residence of Stuart Billings' uncle and guardian, Oliver Halpin, where the deceased made his home for the last two years.'

Lash looked up at Remington and tapped the last paragraph of the story. "Who got the money?"

"What money?"

"Billings' money."

"Oh, that," said Remington, "that's another story. There wasn't any money."

Lash blinked in surprise. "But all this business about his father being the banker, the leading merchant and all that."

"He was, but that's why he committed suicide."

"Who committed suicide?"

"Ralph Billings. He put his money into a railroad — the Western Illinois and Davenport Short Line and then they didn't get a franchise. His brother-in-law, Oliver Halpin — Senior, that is — had to dig down into his own pocket to bury him. And then he had young Stuart on his hands for two years."

Lash stared at the newspaperman for a moment, then bent over and reread the account once more. "You say this is what Sam Carter copied down?"

"No, I didn't say that. I said he copied something from the paper about three-quarters of the way through this volume. But in view of what happened to Sam Carter, I assume this was the item."

"But you're not sure?"

"No, of course not. But I've gone through the volume from here on and there isn't anything else that pertains to the Billingses and the Halpins."

Lash closed the book. "When did Halpin, Senior, die?"

"I was going to look that up, but hadn't got around to it yet. As nearly as I remember, it was eight-ten years after Stuart Billings. Oliver Junior and George were around twenty-one, I think. At least, Ollie was."

"And Mrs. Halpin?"

"She died before her husband."

Lash frowned and started to open the bound volume of the *Mt. Miller Gazette*. Then he closed it again. It would take too much time.

"Thanks," he said.

Remington looked at him quizzically. "You got something out of that item?"

"Yes. I learned that Stuart Billings died."

The newspaper publisher grimaced. "I thought you were going to co-operate."

"I am — as soon as I get something to co-operate about."

"You'll keep me posted?"

Lash shrugged and went to the door. Outside, he climbed into Harry Clyde's car. "Where's the local telephone office?"

Clyde backed the car away from the curb, shot it to the next corner and turned right on the cross street, which was a business block containing the local Bijou Theatre. At the next corner he stopped before a two-story brick building. "Upstairs."

Lash got out and climbed the stairs to the telephone office. He found a switchboard not much larger than fair-sized offices use in cities. A woman of about fifty was at the switchboard.

"I want to put in a call to Hollywood, California," he said. "Granite two, one-one-two-seven . . . "

The operator scribbled the number on a pad, then looked sharply at Lash. "Your name?"

"Simon Lash."

She exclaimed, "Oh — I called that number a couple of times last night."

"That's right."

She indicated a booth at the side of the room. "Will you take the call there?"

Lash entered the booth and had scarcely taken the receiver off the hook than the Los Angeles operator was dialing his home number. Eddie Slocum answered promptly.

"What's happened, Eddie?" Lash asked. He glanced through the glass door and saw the operator's head bent in a listening attitude. He'd expected that.

"The cops were here, chief," Eddie replied. "The lieutenant was awfully sore that you blew out of town."

"I can imagine. What else?"

"That girl came back. Mrs. — "

"Brown?" Lash said quickly.

"Yeah, sure. She said — "

"Never mind, Eddie. I'll call you later. Sit tight."

He hung up the receiver and opened the door of the booth. The operator looked up at him, her face flushed.

Lash smiled at her. "Sorry."

"I beg your pardon?"

"I said, sorry I couldn't talk more."

"It's three dollars and sixty cents, just the same."

Lash brought out a roll of bills, below the level of the railing, so the operator could not see them. He peeled off a fifty, put the roll in his pocket and tendered the bill to the operator.

"I'm sorry," she said, "I don't have change for that."

"I'm afraid it's the smallest I have."

"Nobody in Mt. Miller carries bills like that. And we keep almost no money here in the evening."

"Well, what am I going to do?"

"You'll have to get change somewhere. I can't leave here myself."

"But if I go out to get change, how do you know I'll come back?"

She frowned. "You wouldn't do that, would you?"

"The man who was working for me — the one who made the calls to me last night, did he pay you for them?"

"They were collect calls."

"Oh, you remember them?"

"How many calls to Hollywood do you think I make from here in a week?"

"I haven't any idea — fifteen or twenty, maybe?"

"I made exactly three this week, which is three more than I made in the last six months."

"Three? Sam Carter phoned me only twice."

"The other was — somebody else's."

"Somebody calling a movie star?"

"Of course not. It was — I mean, I can't tell you that."

Lash hesitated. "There's nobody here but us — and the mice."

The operator looked at him frankly. "You're a detective, Mr. Lash, aren't you?"

He nodded. "So was Sam Carter. You heard about him?"

"That he was killed by George Halpin's bull?"

A light showed up on the board; she made a connection and turned back to Lash. He said: "He wasn't killed by a bull. He was murdered."

This made her eyes widen in surprise. "But I thought . . . "

"He got a phone call at the hotel right after midnight. He went out and — got murdered."

She stared at him a moment, then shock registered in her already widened eyes. "But that call was from . . . "

She stopped and Lash prodded softly: "Yes . . . ?"

"It was the . . . " Again she stopped, recalling her official position. Lash looked at her steadily.

Another light on the switchboard saved her. She made a connection, said, "Yes, Mr. Benton, right away." She made another connection, said: "Mt. Miller, Illinois, calling New York . . . " She shot a quick glance over her shoulder, realizing that Lash was taking this all in, then returned her glance to her switchboard. "New York, Plaza five, three-three-four-three . . . Just a moment, Mr. Benton calling . . . " She made another connection, then looked up at Lash, her face fiery.

"I didn't know Claude Benton was in

town," Lash said, casually.

"He's staying at the hotel. Now, see here, Mr. Lash, I don't know what you're trying to get out of me, but in my position — "

"I know," said Lash, "but you keep records of calls here and I may have to subpoena them."

"Subpoena!" she exclaimed.

"And I may have to subpoena you, too."

"Me — what for?"

He shrugged. "It's only natural *you* might listen in on a conversation — accidentally, of course. But you'd have to testify to that — under oath."

"In — in court?"

"Of course."

"But I don't understand — nobody's been — I mean, nobody's been arrested for anything."

"Not yet. But somebody's always arrested in a murder case."

She didn't like that, but whether she would have talked, Lash didn't know, for at that moment the door opened and Harry Clyde came in.

"Hello, Aunt Emma," he said. Then he

signaled to Lash that he had something to say to him.

Lash said: "You wouldn't have three dollars on you, Harry?"

"The only money I've got is what you gave me."

Lash shrugged and reached into his pocket. He produced three singles and found sixty cents in change. He handed the money to the telephone operator. She realized then that the fifty-dollar bill had been a ruse of some kind.

Her lips pressed together in a thin, taut line. "You behave yourself, Harry," she called after Clyde as he followed Lash out of the door.

On the stairs, going down to the street, Clyde said: "George Halpin just went into the movie. He'll be there two hours."

"He lives alone out on his farm?"

"Yes. That's why I thought you might want to know about him going to the movie."

"A man after my own heart, Harry."

They got into the jalopy and a moment later were turning back to Main Street. On the highway at the end of town, Clyde turned left and rolled past the plant of the Midwest Consolidated Dairies.

It was quite dark by this time and the old Halpin house looked even bigger than during daylight. Clyde turned the car from the road into the lane leading up to the house and a dog began barking furiously.

"Oh-oh," said Lash. "Where was he before?"

"In the house, I guess. But don't worry . . . "

He shut off the motor and a big police dog charged up, barking.

Clyde said: "Oscar, old boy!" and the dog began wagging his tail. Clyde got out of the car and patted the dog.

Lash ventured out of the car, then. "You know all the dogs around here?"

"Comes in handy."

Lash said: "Is the telephone operator really your aunt?"

"Yep. She knows everything that goes on in this town. But she doesn't tell what she knows."

"I wish I knew about a telephone call Sam Carter got last night."

"You tried pumping her?"

177

"I did — but I didn't get the answer."

"You won't."

Lash coughed. "I thought maybe you could get it."

"Aunt Emma thinks I'm a bad boy."

They approached the house, the dog following. Clyde tried the front door. "Locked," he announced.

Lash looked at the keyhole. "Locked with what?"

"A key, I guess."

"You mean a thing like this?"

Lash took an old-fashioned skeleton key out of his pocket, put it into the lock and turned it. "This kind of lock wouldn't keep out a smart ten-year-old boy."

He pushed open the door. There was an electric light switch just within the door, but he hesitated. "What about lights?"

"George Halpin hasn't got two friends in the county," Clyde replied. "Nobody'll stop in here on a visit, if that's what you mean."

16

LASH pressed the light switch and surveyed about as dingy a room as he had ever seen. The room was a large one and had evidently been the parlor in another era. But now it was used as a bedroom, living room and dining room.

There was a couch at one side of the room on which were dumped ragged blankets and quilts. Overalls, boots and old shirts were scattered about the room and dirty dishes were piled on a table.

"Not much of a housekeeper," Clyde observed.

"Didn't he ever get married?"

"I heard he got married when he was twenty-one or two, but his wife only lived a year or two. He never married again."

"This house has been in the Halpin family a long time?"

"Far's I know nobody else ever owned it before."

Lash went to a door and reaching it, switched on the light. He turned it out again. The room was the kitchen and dirtier even than the other room.

He tried a closed door and found that it opened into a bedroom, which by contrast to the other two rooms was practically immaculate. The room had a musty odor and had evidently been closed for a long time. A narrow staircase led to the upper floor. Lash looked at it dubiously, then finally decided to venture up.

Threadbare carpeting covered the stairs, but dust rose as Lash climbed. George Halpin evidently didn't use the upstairs very often. In fact, from appearances he had confined his living to the two rooms downstairs.

There was a light switch at the head of the stairs and Lash flicked it, revealing a narrow hall with four doors opening off it. Three bedrooms. In one of them Stuart Billings had died. But which one?

Lash opened one of the doors, groped for a light switch but failed to find it. He struck a match and found a cord dangling from the ceiling. He pulled on it and a single, unshaded bulb lit up.

There was an old-fashioned wooden bedstead in the room, covered with a musty-looking quilt, a chest of drawers and a stand containing a cracked pitcher and bowl. It was not a very attractive room. Lash opened a couple of the drawers and found them empty.

He took another look around the room, then pulled on the light cord and returning to the hall, tried the next bedroom — a room about twice the size of the first and containing a massive wooden bedstead.

The bedroom downstairs for Mr. and Mrs. Halpin, the big bedroom for the two Halpin boys, Oliver and George, the little one for their 'guest,' Stuart Billings.

There was a small bookshelf under the window in the 'boys'' room. It contained fifteen or twenty incredibly dusty books. Lash stooped to look at them, then dropped to one knee.

The shelf contained a half dozen Harry Castlemon books, two or three Oliver Optics, a Henty — and four by Horatio Alger. The titles were *Ragged Dick*, *Ben The Luggage Boy*, *Phil The Fiddler* and

Victor Vane. But there was no *Ralph Raymond's Heir*.

Lash took out the copy of *Ragged Dick* and flicked the dust off with a handkerchief. There was an inscription in it: '*To my young friend, Oliver Halpin, with the compliments of Horatio Alger, Jr. December 25, 1868*.'

Oliver Halpin, Senior.

Lash put the book back and took down the first of the six Castlemon books — all of which had uniform bindings. The title was *Frank The Young Naturalist*, and it, too, was inscribed, '*To Oliver Halpin, with the best wishes of H. C. Castlemon (Chas. A. Fosdick), January 10, 1865*.'

Presentation copies of first editions.

"Damn," said Lash under his breath.

He looked at two of the other books, *Phil The Fiddler* and *Victor Vane*. The first was also a presentation copy, but the latter had a blank fly page.

He returned the books to the shelf and got to his feet.

He left the room and encountered Harry Clyde, sitting on the top step.

"Find anything?"

Lash shook his head and tried the door

of the third room. It was locked and he produced his skeleton key. When he opened the door a wave of stale, musty air assailed his nostrils.

The room was a storeroom and had apparently been shut up for many years. It contained several ancient trunks on which the dust was a half inch thick.

A few moth-eaten shreds of clothing hung from nails in the wall. Three trunks were piled one on top of another. The bottom one was a well-made, iron-riveted affair. Lash, flicking away dust with his handkerchief, saw initials R.B., Ralph Billings.

He called: "Harry, give me a hand."

Clyde came into the room and looked curiously at Lash. Lash stepped to the trunks. "I want to take a peek at the bottom one."

They lifted off the two trunks and then Lash examined the lock of the bottom trunk. It was locked and so corroded with rust that he doubted if a key would unlock it.

"You want to open that?" Clyde asked.

"Yes, but I don't think I have a key that'll work it."

"Then how about this . . . ?" Clyde asked. He drew back his foot and gave the lock a violent kick. The lock as well as a section of the trunk shattered.

"Well, that's one way of doing it," Lash remarked.

He raised the lid of the trunk with some effort and found some amazingly well-preserved boy's clothing. The trunk had been airtight and the clothing undoubtedly mothproofed when stored away.

"Stuart Billings' clothes," he said aloud.

Clyde frowned uneasily. "The guy's been dead forty-five years."

Gingerly Lash picked up a jacket, shook it out and thrust a hand into a pocket. It was empty, but in moving the jacket, he thought he heard the rustle of paper and tried the inside pocket. His fingers encountered paper and he drew out a square envelope . . . a well-worn envelope, with a smudged inscription: '*For Stuart.*'

Clyde, peering over Lash's shoulder, exclaimed: "Jeez!"

Lash drew a deep breath and extracted

the contents of the envelope. It was a letter, written in ink, that had received much handling before being stowed away here in this trunk. The letter read:

My dear son:

You've had the greatest shock you will ever have in your life, but I know you have not let it hurt you too much. You wouldn't be my son, if you had. You may not understand now, but keep this letter and in time, read it again. You will understand better then, and you will know that I did everything for you. I gambled — and I lost. I am sorry, for your sake, but trust your uncle.

Good-bye, my son,
Ralph Billings
October 15, 1899

Lash handed the letter to Harry Clyde. The latter glanced through it, then handed it roughly back to Lash and walked out of the room. Lash could hear him clumping down the stairs.

Lash refolded the letter, put it back into the jacket and replaced the jacket

185

in the trunk. Then he closed the trunk and, switching out the electric light bulb, left the room. He relocked the door with his key and was heading for the stairs, when Harry Clyde's voice suddenly rang out:

"Somebody's coming!"

Lash took one mighty leap for the stairs and descended them three at a time. As he reached the living room, headlights shone in his eyes.

"We're sunk," Clyde exclaimed.

Outside, a voice called, "Hello, the house!"

Lash drew a deep breath, went to the door and opened it. "Mr. Halpin?" he called.

Sheriff Walters' voice replied: "Who's that?"

Then he got out of his car and came forward. He was almost at the porch before he recognized Lash. "Simon Lash!" he cried.

"Yes," Lash replied. "I just stopped by to see Mr. Halpin, but he doesn't seem to be at home."

The sheriff cocked his head to one side and came up on the porch. He looked past Lash at Harry Clyde in the doorway. "You, Harry."

"Hello," Clyde said casually.

The sheriff glowered at Lash. "How'd you get in the house?"

"Why, the door was unlocked. We knocked and when there was no answer I tried the door — "

"And the light was on?"

"Yes."

"Upstairs, too?"

"No, when I couldn't find him downstairs, I thought I'd take a peek upstairs."

"Do they do that in California, Lash?" the sheriff asked sarcastically. "Perfect strangers stop at a man's house, open the door and go upstairs to look for somebody?"

"In view of what happened here last night — "

"That didn't happen at the house!" Walters snapped.

"Maybe not, but just the same, a man was killed here yesterday and when I came up and couldn't find Halpin, well ... I thought something might have happened to him — "

"Halpin's at the movie in town."

"Oh, is he?"

The sheriff attacked Harry Clyde suddenly. "And you, Harry — you didn't mind looking through a man's house, did you?" He shifted back to Lash. "Know anything about this man, Lash?"

"I hired him to drive me around."

"You picked the right man for the job. Harry's served time in the state penitentiary."

"Is that so?" Lash asked evenly.

"It's burglary!" the sheriff cried. "That's what it is."

"My pockets are loaded with jewelry," Lash said.

The sheriff whipped back his right hand, then stopped at his hip. He looked suspiciously at Lash. "Turn out your pockets."

Lash pulled out his pockets one at a time, removing whatever contents he had in the particular pocket and showing it to the sheriff. The result seemed to prove his innocence of the burglary charge, but the sheriff didn't like it.

"I dunno whether a man has to steal

something or not to make it burglary. I know doggone well it ain't right for someone to break into a man's house — "

"We didn't break in — the door was open," Harry Clyde said sullenly.

"But you knew George wasn't home!"

"We knew nothing of the kind," Lash declared. "The light was on and we assumed — "

"I doubt that the light was on. George don't leave it on when he goes to town." The sheriff scowled. "If George wants to make something of this — "

"If he does," Lash said quickly, "you know where to find me."

"Where?"

"At the hotel."

The sheriff hesitated and Lash crowded his point. "Don't worry, I'm not leaving this town until I find out how Sam Carter was really killed. And who killed him."

That did it. The sheriff turned away, but whirled back for a parting shot at Harry Clyde. "You, Harry, with your record, I should think you'd know enough not to get into trouble."

"Sheriff," said Harry Clyde, "go to hell."

The sheriff started to waggle an admonishing finger at Clyde, then thought better of it and, muttering, went to his car. Clyde reached back into Halpin's house, switched out the light and closed the door. He and Lash descended the porch steps and waited for the sheriff to back and turn with his car.

Then they both climbed into Clyde's car and followed, but more slowly.

"Sorry, Clyde," said Lash, as they drove back to Mt. Miller.

"It's all right. The sheriff doesn't worry me." Clyde drove in silence for a moment, then added: "Nobody does."

He did not speak again until they were rolling down Main Street. Then he asked: "Where, now?"

"The hotel."

At the hotel Clyde shut off the ignition and slumped down in his seat. Lash got out and went into the hotel. The dining room, he noted, was closed, but there were still two or three of the town loafers hanging about.

The hotel clerk was unoccupied at the moment, if you call reading a *Racing Form* doing nothing. Lash went up to him. "You remember my friend, Sam Carter?"

The clerk regarded him uneasily over the *Racing Form*. "There was a man by that name registered here yesterday."

"He got a telephone call shortly after midnight."

"He *made* one around twelve," the clerk said. "A long distance call to California . . ."

"To me. Then he got a call a few minutes later and went out."

"He was found dead in George Halpin's pasture." The clerk smiled faintly. "So he *must* have gone out."

"Who," said Lash, "was the call from?"

"I don't know's he got a call."

"He received a call," Lash said flatly.

"Well, he didn't tell me who the call was from."

"The phone's right here on your desk. *You* answered it and called Carter."

"I didn't call him — he was sitting right there in that chair."

"All right, but you answered the phone."

"I usually do answer the phone when it rings."

"Who was it called Carter?"

"Why, I don't know. He didn't say . . . "

"Didn't you recognize the voice?"

The clerk winced at that. "No."

"But you know it was a man."

"I — I don't really remember."

"You said *he* a moment ago."

"So I did. I guess it was a man, then."

"Well, we've got that far," Lash said grimly. "It was a man who telephoned Sam Carter. Now, think again — did you recognize the voice?"

"No, I didn't."

"Was the voice George Halpin's?"

The clerk frowned uneasily.

"You're barking up the wrong tree, Mr. Lash. George Halpin didn't kill Sam Carter. It was his bull."

"Sam Carter was from the city," Lash said. "I don't think he'd go into bull pastures in the middle of the night. Which reminds me, how did Sam get around town?"

"Oh, he had a car. Came out here in one."

"Where's the car now?"

"Sheriff took it over, I guess."

Lash drew a deep breath. "What time did Claude Benton arrive in town yesterday?"

"About three." The clerk winced. "I mean, I — I don't remember. I don't come on duty until five-thirty."

"Is Benton in the hotel now?"

The clerk swallowed hard. "Why, uh, I don't really know . . . "

"I'll run up and see. What's the number of his room . . . ?"

"Why, uh, come to think of it, Mr. Benton's gone to bed. Said he, uh, didn't want to be disturbed."

"Would you rather I'd just go upstairs and knock on every door until I found his room?"

"No-no, don't do that. Uh, it's number sixteen — sixteen and seventeen."

Lash walked to the stairs and climbed to the second floor. Numbers sixteen and seventeen were connecting rooms. Lash rapped on the door of number sixteen.

"Yes?" called a voice inside the room.

"Mr. Benton, I'd like to talk to you."

"Who is it?"

"Simon Lash — from Hollywood, California."

There was silence inside the room, then the door was suddenly whisked open. Claude Benton was a rather handsome man in his late fifties, although he looked younger. He'd had a good many facial massages in his time. The eyes that looked at Lash were steely.

"What are you doing in Mt. Miller?" he asked coldly.

"I was just going to ask you that question."

"This is my home town."

Benton was still blocking the doorway. Lash made a slight gesture with his hand. "Can I come in?"

Benton stepped aside and Lash entered. The suite consisted of two bedrooms, with connecting door — a shabbily furnished suite, but the best that the town afforded. Benton swung the door shut.

"Your son came up to see me in Hollywood," Lash said. "And so did your daughter-in-law — "

"My *former* daughter-in-law," Benton corrected.

"She wanted me to find a book for her — a Horatio Alger book."

"You called me about an Alger book," Benton snapped. "What's it all about?"

"Why, it's a book you owned once."

"I told you that."

"So you did. I also asked if you remembered where *you* got that book."

"I don't."

"Did you get it from Stuart Billings?"

"Stuart Billings!" exclaimed Benton. "He's been dead fifty years."

"Forty-five. You still remember him?"

"Why shouldn't I? He was my cousin."

Lash said quietly: "Ollie Halpin's your cousin, too, then?"

"In a way, I suppose. It's pretty distant, though. As a matter of fact, my mother was a cousin of Ralph Billings — Stuart's father. I called him cousin, but he was a second cousin, actually."

"I see. Whereas Mrs. Halpin was the sister of Mrs. Billings."

"That's right."

Lash nodded. "Did you get the book

from Stuart Billings?"

"I told you I don't know."

"You said you didn't remember. But you *could* have gotten it from him?"

Benton shook his head. "I doubt it. Although I knew Stuart — and was related to him — the times I visited at his house, you could count on the toes of one foot." He scowled. "My father was the blacksmith and Ralph Billings was the village squire." He hesitated, then went on sardonically, "We were poor relations."

"Until Ralph Billings also became poor."

"He didn't . . . " Benton stopped and looked sharply at Lash. "Where did you learn all this about the Billings family?"

"I've been in Mt. Miller for over two hours."

"Snooping around, eh? Well, then you know all about the Billingses."

"I know that Ralph Billings lost all his money and then shot himself."

"He didn't shoot himself. He took poison."

"But he did commit suicide — and he

lost all his money?"

"He took a flier in railroads — and guessed wrong."

"And he lost *all* of his money?"

"Yes."

"When you say all of his money, you mean *all* — and not just figuratively speaking?"

"I mean all," Benton said grimly. "Including some money he borrowed from the bank . . . "

"Stole?"

"They called it borrowed. And they took even his house, after his death. There was nothing left." Benton grinned cruelly. "It was the biggest thing this town had ever seen. And Stuart went to live with the Halpins — they took him in, to keep him from going to the poor farm."

"He got along all right with the Halpins?"

"Are you kidding? Old Oliver Halpin was tighter than a door that hasn't been open in sixteen years. He worked the pants off Stuart. My old man was no angel, especially when he was drunk, which was most of the time, but at least we ate in our house. Well, so did the Halpins, if they raised it on the farm, but I guess it was mostly cabbage and carrot soup for Stuart Billings."

"Yet Oliver Halpin wasn't a poor man."

"What makes you think he wasn't?"

"He had an eighty-acre farm — and a dairy."

Benton's lips curled in disgust. "That two-bit dairy!"

"Young Oliver made three million dollars out of it."

"He didn't make it from the dairy."

"Well, from the dried-milk business. But he got his start with the dairy."

"I got my start in a blacksmith shop, but I didn't make my pile from it."

"You worked in a department store in Chicago, didn't you?"

"For ten years. Then I started my own store. When I sold the Chicago store, I went to New York —"

"And you've done all right."

"You can get my history from *Who's Who*."

"I did."

Benton grunted. "Then you know all

about me?" He yawned. "Think I'll turn in early tonight."

Lash ignored the hint. He said: "Have you seen Sterling Knox recently, Mr. Benton?"

Benton's face twisted angrily. "Knox is dead, Lash! I know that as well as you do. And I know that that's why you've come to Mt. Miller."

"No, that isn't why I came to Mt. Miller. Knox was murdered in California. I'll find his murderer there. I came to Mt. Miller because a man named Sam Carter was murdered *here*. And Sam Carter was working for me . . ."

"Carter wasn't murdered."

"How do you know he wasn't?"

"He was killed by a bull."

"Did you see the bull kill him?"

Benton stepped around Lash and whipped open the door. "That ends this!"

Lash looked at the open door, but made no move to step through it. He said calmly: "It was almost midnight, Eastern time, when I talked to you on the phone, the night before last. You must have left New York shortly afterwards to get here by three o'clock yesterday afternoon."

"I left New York at eight o'clock. I got to Chicago at twelve o'clock — Central time. I came out from Chicago by train. At precisely five minutes after three I entered these rooms — which I had reserved two weeks ago."

"You reserved these rooms beforehand?"

"Ask Benny, the man at the desk, if you don't believe me."

"In other words, you had this trip *planned?*"

Benton laughed harshly. "Mr. Lash, are you laboring under the impression that my trip to Mt. Miller was a sudden one — caused by your phone call to me in New York?"

"I had such an idea — yes."

"Well, forget it."

"And I suppose," Lash went on, "your son's sudden trip from Las Vegas to Los Angeles was also planned beforehand?"

"I know nothing of my son's movements. For all I know, he's still in Las Vegas."

"He wasn't yesterday."

Benton shrugged. "My son is thirty-one

200

years old. He doesn't ask my permission when he makes a trip."

Lash finally went through the opened door. He heard the door close as he descended the stairs.

17

DOWN in the lobby, only one loafer remained. Benny, the night clerk, still had the *Racing Form* on the desk in front of him, but he wasn't reading it. His face wore a rather pained expression, which could be either an attack of indigestion or Benny, thinking, about something unpleasant.

Lash went up to him.

"I understand Mr. Benton reserved his suite of rooms two weeks ago."

"Yeah, that's right."

"By telegram."

"I don't know how he reserved them. Mr. Hale, the owner of the hotel, told me Mr. Benton would be out and to keep those rooms for him."

"He comes here frequently?"

"'Bout once every twenty years."

Lash gave the clerk a look of disgust and walked out of the hotel. Harry Clyde was still behind the wheel of his car. His eyes were closed when Lash came up, but he wasn't sleeping.

Lash got in beside him. "The newspaper office."

Clyde started the car, made a quick U-turn and headed down Main Street.

Remington, the newspaper publisher, was still in his office. He had a huge stack of bound file copies on his desk and was going through them. His eyes lit up when Lash came into the office.

"Look what you've got me doing!"

Lash noted the date of the file Remington had opened. 1898. Remington saw his glance. "The year of the big crash," he said. "Billings, small-town tycoon, taken by Chicago financiers." He slapped the newspaper. "It's all here, but my old man was afraid of libel and handled the city boys pretty carefully. The first announcement of Billings' railroad affiliations said the group — that's Billings and the city slickers — already had the railroad franchise."

"I'd imagine that'd be the first thing they'd get."

"You'd think so, wouldn't you?" Remington said. "And from what I gather about Ralph Billings he was a pretty cagey lad. I don't think he'd sink two hundred thousand into a scheme unless he looked it over pretty carefully."

"Is that what he went for — two hundred thousand dollars?"

Remington nodded. "Which was a lot of money in those days — and a helluva lot for a man in a town of eight hundred population which is what Mt. Miller had in those days."

"Only it wasn't all his own money. Some of it belonged to the bank."

"Where'd you get that?"

"Claude Benton."

"You've talked to him?"

"I just came from there. He told me he was a second cousin of Stuart Billings."

"I could have told you that myself."

"What else can you tell me?"

"About Claude Benton?"

"About Claude Benton, the Halpins, the Billingses — Sterling Knox."

"Sterling Knox?"

"Yes."

"I don't see the connection between Sterling Knox and — well, Claude Benton."

"Murder," Lash said quietly.

Remington looked narrowly at Lash for a moment, then suddenly he inhaled softly. "Of course — you're investigating Sterling Knox's death in California! You sent Sam Carter here on some angle . . . and *he* was murdered."

"You've got the picture. Sam Carter was digging up information for me — information I needed to solve the murder of Sterling Knox. He was killed and no matter what anyone says, no matter what it looks like, nobody will ever convince me that Carter wasn't murdered."

"Can I quote you on that?"

"In your local paper?"

Remington grimaced, "The Chicago papers. I'll telephone them the story."

"Go ahead." Lash indicated the phone. "Now."

Remington needed no further urging. He picked up the phone and said, "Emma, get me the Chicago *Daily Globe*, will you?" A moment later he had the newspaper and asked for the city editor. When he got him, he said: "This is Chester Remington, publisher of the *Mt. Miller Gazette*. We've had a murder here and I thought you might be interested in the story. It involves some rather big people." He scowled. "No; not big Mt. Miller people. Claude Benton of Benton's Department Store, in New York . . . Fine . . . Well, here's the story. A man named Sterling Knox — yes, Knox's Shoe Stores of Chicago — was murdered yesterday in Hollywood, California . . . You've had that story? The connection is that Knox's home town is Mt. Miller, Illinois. And Claude Benton's, too. Anyway, a famous California detective named Simon Lash was engaged to investigate the murder of Sterling Knox, in California. He got in touch with a private detective from Chicago — a man named Sam Carter. Well, Carter was killed here last night, within six hours after arriving in town. No — no, the sheriff called it an accidental death. He was found in a pasture, gored by a bull . . . "

At that point Lash slipped out of the office, sprang into Clyde's car at the curb. "The telephone office — quick!"

Clyde seemed a little surprised, but shot the car around the corner, passed the Bijou Theatre and came to a

206

squealing stop in front of the telephone building.

Lash dashed up the stairs, opened the door and caught the night phone operator, hunched over her board, her eyes squinted in thought, as she listened in on a conversation. At Lash's entry she reacted in surprise and shot a quick glance down at her plugs.

"Aunt Emma," Lash said, "are you listening in on Remington's Chicago call?"

"I beg your pardon!" the operator exclaimed. Then she became indignant. "See here, Mr. Lash, I want you to understand" — and as she talked her fingers pulled out a plug from the switchboard — "I'm not in the habit of listening in on other people's conversations."

"You had somebody else plugged in on that talk," Lash accused.

"I did not!"

But her face showed her guilt.

"Who was it?"

"I don't know what you're talking about and if you don't stop insulting me I shall call the sheriff." To give weight to her threat, she picked up a plug and pointed it threateningly at the switchboard.

Lash laughed and left the room.

Down on the sidewalk, Harry Clyde said: "George Halpin just left the movie."

"For all of me, he can go home and have a good night's sleep. If he's got a clear conscience."

"So far," said Clyde, "I haven't asked you just what you're trying to find out, Mr. Lash."

"I'm trying to find out who killed Sam Carter."

"Is that why you've been looking through old newspapers?"

"Yes."

Clyde toyed with the steering wheel. "It ain't any of my business and you can tell me to shut my mouth, but maybe I could help you."

"You could find out from your Aunt Emma who it was telephoned Carter at the hotel last night, right after midnight."

Clyde sighed. "I guess I can't help you then, because Aunt Emma wouldn't tell me the right time. But if it was about Stuart Billings — "

"What do you know about Stuart Billings?"

"I've lived in Mt. Miller all my life."

"But Stuart Billings died before you were born."

"Sure enough, but you grow up in a small town like this where not much happens and you pick up things that happened long before your time. Like murder . . . ."

"Murder?"

"Mt. Miller never had a murder in all the years it's been in existence. Not an out in the open murder. But there was always talk about the Billingses."

"That Stuart was murdered?"

"Oliver Halpin never had more'n one pot to cook in, then after Stuart Billings died he bought a lot of dairy cattle and built up a new dairy building — talk like that, you know. I grew up on it."

"What other talk was there, Harry? About the Billings money, for instance?"

"Old Man Billings? He was supposed to be the richest man in these parts."

"But he lost his money. Or didn't people believe that he lost all of his money?"

"People don't usually put all their eggs in one basket, do they?"

"No," said Lash thoughtfully. "They don't."

"You were searching George Halpin's old stuff . . . I thought maybe you'd like to take a look at the old Billings place."

"It's still standing?"

Clyde nodded. "Yep! And what's more nobody's lived in it since Ralph Billings killed himself. The bank took the place over and tried to rent it but nobody around here would take it. And then after a few years the place ran down pretty much and it got a bad reputation."

"Haunted?"

"People claim they saw old Ralph Billings walking around. Lights at night, stuff like that. I spent a night there when I was sixteen or seventeen."

"Even though you knew it was supposed to be haunted?"

"I had a dollar bet." He started the motor of the car. "You want to run out?"

"What about light?"

Clyde pointed to a battered glove

compartment. "Flashlight in there."

"Then let's go."

A few minutes later they were out of town. They drove past the plant of the Midwest Consolidated Dairies, past George Halpin's farmhouse, where there were lights upstairs as well as on the first floor. A mile beyond the Halpin place, Clyde began to slacken speed.

Lash searched for the Billings house, but saw only a grove of trees on the right. Clyde stopped his car. "It's in among those trees — and we've got to walk."

Lash looked at the barbed wire fence beside the road. "That isn't a bull pasture, is it?"

Clyde smiled thinly. "It's a pasture — belongs to a farmer named Holtznagle, but he hasn't got a bull."

Lash opened the glove compartment and found a rather surprisingly large flashlight. He took it out and looked toward the black mass of trees that were at least two hundred feet from the highway.

"I don't think this flashlight is going to make enough light," he said uneasily. "I guess I'll come back in the morning."

"I told you the reason I did that year in the state pen, didn't I?"

"For holding up a traveling salesman."

Clyde nodded. "Fella I was driving around like this. You know how much money I got?"

"I'm not in a guessing mood."

"It was thirty-two bucks."

"A small-town bad man," Lash said, bitterly.

"Yeah," admitted Clyde. "I got a reputation. I been out of the Big Place over a year and you know how many days work I've had since then? N–o–n–e, none. Give a dog a bad name . . ."

"I know a name for a dog," Lash said.

"Very funny," said Clyde, without humor. He gestured with the gun. "Get out. And put down the flashlight."

Lash dropped the flashlight to the seat of the car and climbed out. He looked up and down the road, but of course no headlights were approaching from either direction. There never are, when you want to see them.

Clyde got out of the car on his own

side. He gripped the flashlight in his left hand, flicked it on and pointed it at the barbed wire fence.

"Let's go."

"What for?"

"Because I said so."

"I can give you my money right here."

"And somebody comes along and picks you up and I hardly get back to town than the sheriff's after me? Uh-uh, get going."

Lash stumbled over the drainage ditch and caught his coat on a barb in the wire, but finally got through into the field. Clyde kept the flashlight on him and fell in a few feet behind Lash.

Lash said over his shoulder: "You won't be far enough away by morning, Clyde, because no matter where you go, I'll get you."

"Maybe," said Clyde. "And maybe not. I don't think you'll ever see me after tonight."

Lash didn't like the last statement. It could have a double meaning.

He continued on across the field. As they neared the trees, Clyde shut off his flashlight. Lash risked a glance over his shoulder and saw the headlights of a car coming from the direction of Mt. Miller.

"Stand still," Clyde ordered. "They won't see us from the road if we don't move."

He put his hand on his hip, the muzzle of his gun depressed, but so that it could be brought up even while pressing the trigger. Lash stood still while the headlights flashed past on the road.

Clyde flicked on the flashlight again. "All right."

Lash resumed his march for the trees and as he approached saw the shadow outline of a house. Clyde let the light play on it a moment; it picked out gaping window frames. Trees had grown up to the very walls of the old place.

As they came up to the house, Clyde said: "Well, I don't see Old Man Billings."

And no sooner had he said the words, than a voice came out of the deserted ruins. "Harry?"

"Yes," Clyde called back promptly.

"A live ghost," Lash observed.

18

A DIM light showed in the building — a kerosene lamp, in one of the rear rooms. Clyde stepped up close behind Lash and prodded him with his revolver.

"The door's unlocked."

Lash brushed away bushes that had grown up in front of the door, found a door hanging on hinges. He maneuvered a passage through it, with Clyde almost stepping on his heels.

Footsteps sounded in one of the rear rooms and then — Sheriff Walters appeared.

"Good evening, Mr. Lash," he said.

"Surprised, aren't you?" Clyde asked.

"Not very," Lash retorted. "Aunt Emma spilled it."

The sheriff stared at Lash. "Emma never told you nothing. She told me she didn't."

"She didn't give you a name," Lash said, "but when I asked her about the

215

call to Sam Carter last night, she started to say it was the sheriff. She didn't say mister or any name, just *the*."

"Could have been the butcher, or the grocer," the sheriff said.

"Only the butcher and the grocer weren't after me — and you were."

The sheriff glowered at Lash for a moment, then stepped back into the adjoining room. Clyde, close beside Lash, prodded him and Lash followed into a larger square room, that had a packing case in the center of the floor. On it stood the lamp.

Clyde shut off his flashlight and stepped back from Lash, so that Lash couldn't reach him by a sudden movement.

Lash said: "I've got three hundred dollars in my pocket, Harry. You can go a long ways with it — and the hundred you've already got. And I won't be going after you."

"You won't, anyway," said Clyde.

"Mr. Lash," said the sheriff, "I'm awfully sorry about all this. Things have been nice and quiet around Mt. Miller for a long time. We've had no crime to speak of — "

"Since Clyde stuck up a traveling salesman.

"That was a little mistake on Clyde's part. The man made such a fuss about it, Clyde had to — well, take the rap, I guess you'd call it. But it was only a year."

"You get the chair for murder."

"Who's talking about murder, Lash?"

"I am."

"Sam Carter was killed by a bull. Everybody's satisfied about that."

"Everybody but all the Chicago newspapers. They're coming out in the morning and calling it murder. And they're saying some things about the sheriff of this county — and about Claude Benton and Oliver Halpin and Sterling Knox. You're going to see more newspaper reporters around Mt. Miller than you ever knew there were — and more big town policemen."

The sheriff stared at Lash. "What're you talking about?"

"Chet Remington — he telephoned all the Chicago papers." He nodded to Clyde. "Aunt Emma can verify that. She was listening in."

"I don't believe it!" snapped the sheriff.

But Clyde looked uneasy. "He was at the telephone office just before we came here — and he went there from the newspaper office."

"What was Remington doing when you left there?" the sheriff demanded.

"He was on the telephone."

"I don't think they'll go for two bull-killings in two days," Lash said.

Harry Clyde exhaled wearily. "I guess we'd better check up, Uncle — "

"Uncle?" exclaimed Lash.

"Aunt Emma's brother — didn't you know?"

"I guess everybody's related to everybody in town," Lash said, bitterly. "I suppose Chet Remington's a cousin?"

"Well, no, that's the only bad part of this," Clyde said, "Chet don't like our family too well. He wanted to be postmaster a couple of years ago and Cousin Milton got the job."

"All right," the sheriff said, "I'll run in and talk to Emma."

"Better take my car," Clyde suggested, "it's out on the road, kind of prominent."

The sheriff scowled at Lash. "Keep your eyes peeled, Harry."

"I can handle him."

The sheriff hesitated, then shrugged and left the room. His footsteps sounded hollowly in the front room, then died as he left the house.

Lash looked at Harry Clyde. "All right to sit down?"

"Against the wall," said Clyde.

Lash walked to the side of the room and sat down on the dirty floor. Clyde crossed so that he was on the far side of the room, a good twenty feet from Lash. The packing case on which the lamp stood was between them, but to one side.

For a few moments they regarded each other across the room. Then Lash said: "This is really the old Billings house?"

"Yep."

"What room did Billings die in?"

Clyde made no reply. Lash said: "Or, didn't he die in the house?"

Clyde shook his head. "I don't know — and I don't care."

"Who's paying for this?" Lash persisted.

"I'm doing it as a favor."

"For your uncle? Well, who's paying him."

"Nobody."

Lash snorted. "He's killing two men for fun?"

Clyde sighed. "Cut it out Lash. I'm not in the mood."

"If it comes to that — neither am I. But I'm not just going to sit here and bite my fingernails."

"Shut up, will you?"

"Were you on the level about that working business, Clyde? That no one in Mt. Miller's given you a job since you came out?"

Clyde grunted a reply that could have meant anything.

"A thousand dollars," Lash said. "You can go a helluva long ways with that."

"You said you've only got three hundred with you."

"I can get the other seven hundred."

"How?"

"I can wire for it."

Clyde made a derisive noise with his mouth. "Three hundred in the hand's good enough for me."

"Uncle's going to let you keep the three hundred?"

"Uncle's getting his."

"Oh — so he *is* being paid!"

Clyde swore. "Damn you, Lash, shut your trap!"

Lash remained silent for about two minutes. Then he said: "How'd you like it at Stateville?"

Clyde suddenly came across the room. He stopped three feet from Lash and looked down. "One more crack, Lash, and I'll kick in your face."

Lash guessed that he had gone far enough. He stayed quiet for almost a half hour. And then a voice called cautiously from somewhere outside the house: "All right, Harry?"

Clyde called back, "All right."

Footsteps sounded at the front of the house. Then the sheriff entered the room. His face showed verification of Lash's report.

"Remington talked to the Chicago papers, all right," the sheriff said. "Emma heard most of it, except for a couple of minutes when he" — nodding to Lash — "was up in the office."

221

"And they're going to say Sam Carter was murdered?"

"They can say it all they want, but they can't prove it. He gets buried tomorrow."

Harry Clyde looked worried. "It's all right for you — you're the sheriff. They can call you a dope for not knowing he wasn't killed by a bull, but me, I'm the only man in Mt. Miller with a record."

"And he'll throw you to the wolves when the going gets rough, Harry," Lash cut in.

Harry Clyde regarded Lash broodingly. The sheriff looked at his nephew and said quickly, "We'll stick together, Harry, don't worry."

"Like he stuck to you the last time," Lash said, "when he let you go to the penitentiary."

"Lash," said the sheriff testily, "keep out of this. Harry, you know I did what I could for you."

"Sure," said Clyde. "Only *I* served the time."

"And *you'll* do the frying this time," Lash pointed out.

The sheriff came over to Lash. He drew a .38 from his pocket. "I think you've said about enough, Lash," he began. Then Harry Clyde came forward.

"Wait a minute, Uncle, I want to get this settled first . . ."

"It's already settled," the sheriff snapped. "You helped me last night — "

"Yes, but *I* didn't kill Sam Carter."

"Shut up, Harry!" cried the sheriff.

Lash came up from the floor at that moment. The sheriff cried out in alarm and threw down with his .38 and the only thing that saved Lash from that first shot was that the sheriff miscalculated. He assumed that Lash was coming directly at him. And he fired in that direction. But Lash was lunging for the packing case, not the sheriff.

The first shot missed him by feet. Then the sheriff, in whirling, knocked against Harry Clyde and spoiled Clyde's aim. Clyde's bullet whizzed over Lash's back.

Then Lash hit the packing box. He hit it with so much force that the kerosene lamp which stood on it flew clear across the room. It smashed against the wall — and exploded.

Fire lit up the far side of the room, but it only emphasized the darkness on the other side and there Lash was now scuttling for the feet or legs of the sheriff.

Harry Clyde sprang back, looking for a chance to shoot.

Lash clawed at the sheriff, brushed against a leg. The sheriff, trying to leap back, stumbled — and Clyde fired. The bullet intended for Lash struck flesh, but it was the sheriff's flesh.

"Harry!" he screamed. "You shot *me!*"

He toppled backwards, the gun falling from his hand. Lash caught it before it hit the floor. Flame lanced at him again, but Clyde's mis-shot had unnerved him.

Lash fired and saw Clyde recoil from the impact of the bullet. He was about to fire a second time, when the gun fell from Clyde's hand. But Clyde remained on his feet.

"Goddammit!" he said.

The sheriff was thrashing on the floor, sobbing in agony. "You shot me, Harry, you shot me."

Lash slowly rose to his feet. Across the room the fire was spreading rapidly. Kerosene fed the wood of the floor and walls that had been dried almost to the

224

consistency of charcoal by the weather of three generations. It lit up the whole room now.

Clyde's right hand was clutching his chest.

"Goddammit," he said, "I never had a chance."

His knees buckled suddenly and he slid to the floor. But his back supported him against the wall and he remained in a sitting position. The sheriff uttered a final wailing shriek and subsided, although his body still twitched in the final death throes.

Lash moved across the room, although he had to shield the near side of his face from the heat of the flames. "Come on, Harry, I'll get you out of here."

Clyde's face was filmed with perspiration and tears trickled down his cheeks. "Goddammit," he repeated. And then blood gushed from his mouth and he fell sidewards. His eyes remained open and staring.

Lash turned back to the sheriff. His body had stopped twitching. He was dead.

At the door to the front room, Lash

turned and tossed back the sheriff's revolver. Then he walked out of the house.

Halfway to the highway, he looked back. The entire house was ablaze.

He was crawling through the barbed wire when headlights came swooping down the highway. Brakes squealed and a sedan stopped. A man stepped quickly out of the car and looked over toward the fire.

"Well, whaddya know," he said, "the old haunted house has finally gone up."

"It's about time," Lash said.

"I guess old Ralph Billings will have to find another place to do his walking."

Headlights appeared from the direction of Mt. Miller. Another car pulled up, then another, and then two cars came together from the other direction.

Lash started walking toward Mt. Miller.

19

IT was eleven o'clock when Lash started down Main Street in Mt. Miller, but there was still a light in the office of the *Mt. Miller Gazette.*

Remington greeted him enthusiastically. "I've made myself a hundred dollars this evening."

"From the Chicago papers?"

"Yep!" He rubbed his hands together gleefully. "They're all sending reporters. This old burg's going to get such a going-over, they'll never get over it."

"I've got another story for you," Lash said. "There's been a fire out at the old Billings house."

"Is that so? Hoboes?"

Lash shrugged. "If you want to let it go at that, I guess you can say hoboes were camped there and accidentally set the place on fire. But if you don't like that story, you can go out there tomorrow, when the ashes are cold and dig around and find yourself two bodies . . . and two guns . . . "

Remington stared at Lash in awe. "Two bodies . . . two guns . . . W-who — are they?"

"Sheriff Walters and Harry Clyde."

The newspaper publisher gasped. "They shot each other?"

"You might say that and when you're writing up their obituaries, give Harry Clyde a break. He was the better man of the two. Walters murdered Sam Carter — and he would have murdered me, tonight, except for Harry Clyde . . . "

Fifteen minutes later, Lash left the newspaper office and walked wearily to the hotel.

There was no one in the lobby except the night clerk, who was hunched over the desk, reading a copy of *Exciting Western Tales*. He looked over his magazine.

"I put your bag in room fourteen," he said.

"I'm not staying," Lash said.

The clerk frowned. "Well, what about the room; you said you wanted it."

"I'll pay for it. Where can I get someone to drive me to Oregon?"

"If you'd been a half hour sooner

you could have driven over with Mr. Benton."

"Benton's gone?"

The clerk nodded. "He wanted to catch the eleven-thirty for Chicago. But you're too late for that."

"When's the next train?"

"Two o'clock. Say — that's the milk train. You might get a ride over to Oregon in the milk truck."

Lash rode to Oregon on the milk truck. He got an hour's sleep on a bench in the waiting room of the Oregon depot and then dozed fitfully sitting up, during the three-hour ride to Chicago.

In Chicago he had breakfast and got a shave at the station barbershop. Then he phoned the airport and found that he could get a California plane in an hour. A taxi took him to the airport and by eight, Central time, Lash was flying over Illinois farmlands.

There were headwinds over the Rockies, but with the two-hour saving in time, the plane settled down at the Burbank Airport at ten minutes after four in the afternoon. Lash slept most of the way. He rode to the Roosevelt Hotel

229

in the airport Cadillac and there got a taxicab, which deposited him in front of his apartment before five o'clock.

The Cross Detective Agency car was parked across the street.

20

LASH unlocked the street door with his key, climbed the stairs to the second floor and opened the door of his library. Eddie Slocum, sprawled on the couch with a *Racing Form*, sprang to his feet.

"Simon!" he cried.

"Hello, Eddie," Lash said easily. "What's new?"

"Plenty! But for the love of Mike, you left here two nights ago, you've been in Illinois and now you're back."

"I had enough of Illinois. I asked you, what's been doing here?"

Eddie Slocum grimaced. "Cops! They've been practically camping here."

"Why?"

"Lieutenant Bailey figures he's got something on you. Something about your fingerprints being in Sterling Knox's room at the Lincoln Hotel."

"What does he figure to do about it — or didn't he say?"

"He's done it." Eddie coughed gently. "He's got a warrant for your arrest."

"Oh, fine, so I'm going to have trouble with the police department." Lash exhaled heavily. "I see our watchman is still camped across the street."

"He's never been gone. But they're getting worried. Somebody calls up about once every two hours and asks for you."

"He doesn't leave a name?"

Eddie Slocum shook his head. "Young Benton was here this morning."

"I saw his father in Mt. Miller."

Eddie exclaimed. "I thought he was in New York."

"He was — then he was in Mt. Miller and unless I'm a mighty bad guesser, he's in Hollywood right now. He left Mt. Miller a couple of hours ahead of me."

Lash went to his desk, looked at a stack of mail on it, then got out his private phone and address book. "It's about time we washed up this Alger book business." He searched for a number, found it and dialed.

A voice on the phone said cautiously: "Hello?"

"Phil Appleton," Lash said.

"Who's calling?"

"Don't be so damn cagey," Lash snapped. "This is Simon Lash."

"Oh," said the voice. "How are you, Simon?"

"Lousy, and I hope you're the same. Look — I want you to do some work for me."

There was a short pause on the other end of the wire, then Phil Appleton said, "Well, I don't know, Simon, I'm pretty busy right now."

"Cut it out, Phil, you're never too busy to make a dirty buck."

"I like a dollar as well as the next man, Simon," retorted Phil Appleton, "but I buy a newspaper every day and there was a piece in the paper yesterday about an eye you hired in Chicago, who went out to some whistle stop and got himself killed."

"Yes, but you didn't read what happened there last night."

"What happened?"

"Make a guess — I've just come back from there."

"I see," said Appleton, "and I s'pose that makes Sam Carter mighty happy."

233

"Phil," Lash said angrily, "do you want this job or don't you?"

"I want a job, all right, but I don't want lead in my stomach. I got a wife and three kids."

"If you get killed," Lash said coldly, "they'll collect your insurance and be better off than they are now."

"That's what you think . . . All right, what's the job?"

"The Cross Agency's got somebody shadowing me. I want to know who they're doing it for."

"That's all, huh?" Appleton said, sarcastically. "They should break the confidence of a client, that's all."

"Cross would double-cross his mother for a fee," Lash said. "Now, can you do it or not?"

"For how much?"

"For fifty dollars . . . "

"Fifty a day, you mean."

"Fifty a day — all right."

"With a guarantee of five days, eh?"

Lash gritted his teeth. "All right, I've got other work for you, but I want that information first of all."

"You'll have it."

Lash slammed the receiver on the phone, but picked it up again instantly. He dialed another number.

A voice said: "Santa Ana Apartments."

"Mr. Oliver Halpin."

A connection was made and Clare Halpin's voice said: "Yes?"

Lash said in a rasping voice: "Mr. Oliver Halpin, please."

"Who's calling?"

"The Los Angeles Police Department."

There was a short pause, then Clare Halpin said, "Just a moment, please."

Oliver Halpin came on the wire. "Oliver Halpin talking."

"Halpin," Lash said, "I thought you might not want your daughter to know I was calling, so I told her the police . . . This is Simon Lash . . . "

"Oh yes," said Halpin, "that's good, Sergeant."

"Can you come to my apartment?"

Halpin hesitated. Then he said: "Very good, Sergeant. And thanks for calling me. I'll — I'll be down in a little while."

Lash hung up and consulted his book again. He was about to dial a third number, when the phone rang. He scooped off the receiver.

"Simon," said the voice of Phil Appleton, "my wife has a no-good nephew who works for Cross. I had him with me for awhile and tried to teach him the business, but it was just like trying to teach a dummy, so when I gave him the breeze he went over — "

"Give me his pedigree in a letter," snapped Lash. "Did you get the information?"

"Yes. I gave the office a buzz and happened to catch Nick in the office — "

"All right, all right," snarled Lash, "who is it?"

"A man named Charles Benton. I never heard of him, but he's apparently got money, because — "

"He's got it, but don't go giving me a history of Charles Benton. I know it."

"Yes? And do you know that Cross has a day and night shift staked out, watching your office."

"I'm not blind, Phil. Now, listen, call up that no-good nephew of yours again. Find out from him where Benton's staying — "

"He's already told me — he's at the Hollywood-Wilshire."

"Good. Now, here's how you earn your five-days' pay. Get over to the Hollywood-Wilshire. Get on Benton's trail — and let him know he's being shadowed. Got that?"

"I got it, but I don't see the sense of shadowing a man if he knows he's being shadowed."

"Because he's a nervous young punk and I want him made more nervous. So he'll do something."

"What?"

"That's what I want to find out. And look — do you know anybody at the Hollywood-Wilshire?"

"Nobody important, just one of the telephone operators. A cousin of my wife's."

"A no-good like your nephew, I suppose? All right, check with her about Benton's phone calls. And, oh yes, find out if Charles Benton's father is staying at the Wilshire — name is Claude Benton."

"Claude Benton? Say — isn't that the New York department store man?"

"Yes. Now get right over to the hotel and call me as soon as you get there."

"Okay, Simon."

Just as Simon Lash hung up, the door buzzer whirred. Lash looked at Eddie Slocum. "Not already?"

"I'll find out."

Eddie darted into the bedroom and returned in a moment. "Yep, it's a police car. Do you want to hide?"

"I doubt if it'd do any good." Lash sighed. "All right, let him in."

Eddie went down the stairs and returned in a moment or two, with Lieutenant Bailey.

"Where the hell've you been?" the detective demanded as he came into the room.

"Are you asking because you want to know, or just because you hope I'll tell you a lie."

"I don't give a damn what you tell me — I *know* where you've been."

"Then why bother asking?"

"Because you had no right to leave town! I warned you — "

"Look," said Lash, wearily, "you've got a warrant for me, haven't you?"

"You're darned tootin' I have!"

"Are you going to serve it?"

"That depends on you."

"Oh, is that so?"

"Explain how your fingerprints got into Sterling Knox's room at the Lincoln Hotel."

"They got there because I was in his room — how else would they get there?"

The lieutenant scowled. "When were you there?"

"The day before he was murdered," Lash replied calmly.

Bailey regarded Lash sharply. "Knox *knew* you were there?"

"Since I wasn't invisible and he wasn't blind I don't see how he could have helped knowing I was there."

The detective grunted. "Well, why were you there?"

"I was trying to get information — naturally."

Lieutenant Bailey took the warrant from his pocket. He held it aloft. "I'm showing you this, Lash, because I know what you're going to say — that you can't be made to reveal a client's name."

"Get ready for a surprise, Lieutenant,"

Lash said evenly. "I'm not going to refuse to tell you my client's name. In fact, I'm going to tell you everything about him. His name is Oliver Halpin . . ."

Lieutenant Bailey stared at Lash in surprise — and mild disappointment. "Uh, who's Oliver Halpin?" he asked.

"He's a man with three million dollars. A retired dried-milk manufacturer, from Mt. Miller, Illinois."

"That burg in Illinois where you spent the last couple of days?"

"So you do know where I was."

"We've got a very fine teletype down at Headquarters. And the Illinois State Police have one, too. They're very much interested in you, in Illinois. In fact, they don't quite like the idea of you leaving there so sudden-like."

"They apparently know where to find me."

"That they do." Lieutenant Bailey rubbed the side of his nose with a long forefinger. "So this Oliver Halpin is from Mt. Miller, Illinois?"

"Which also happens to be Sterling Knox's old home town. Or didn't you find that out yet?"

"I did. Well — go on, about this Oliver Halpin. What'd he hire you for?"

"To find the owner of a book."

The detective cocked his head to one side. "Come again!"

"A book," Lash said. He picked up the copy of *Ralph Raymond's Heir*, from his desk. "A book like this."

The lieutenant came across the room and took the book from Lash's hand. He looked at it blankly. "I had a book like this when I was a kid. I read a lot of these, uh, Horatio Alger books. I think I even read this one."

"You'd have been a backward kid if you hadn't read Horatio Alger, Lieutenant. Not many kids missed them."

"Then what's so wonderful about this book?"

"It's a rare book."

"This? How much is it worth?"

"Ten or fifteen dollars."

The detective screwed up his mouth. "And you say, this Oliver Halpin hired you to find who owned a book like this . . . ?"

"That's right."

"Why?"

"Mr. Oliver Halpin lives at the Santa Ana Apartments. Suppose you ask him that question. I've asked it six times and I've yet to get a satisfactory answer . . . "

The lieutenant opened the copy of *Ralph Raymond's Heir*, turned a few pages, then suddenly looked up at Lash. "On the teletype, they said a private eye named Sam Carter was killed by a bull in a cornfield. The name of the bull's owner stuck in my mind — it was Halpin . . . "

"George Halpin," Lash said. "Oliver's brother."

"The sheriff up there reported it as an accident — "

"It wasn't an accident."

" . . . And the sheriff," Bailey went on, "was found this morning in an old shack out in the country that'd burned down. Him and some guy shot it out."

Bailey looked at Lash and the latter returned his look unflinchingly. It was the lieutenant who dropped his eyes — uneasily. "I'd hate to think what I'm thinking, Lash."

"Along about tomorrow," Lash said, evenly, the Illinois State Police will decide that the sheriff murdered Sam Carter and dumped him into that bull pasture. And they'll probably also decide that the sheriff and a confederate got into a fight and shot it out. They may decide that and announce it or they may decide it and just let the thing drop altogether, since the sheriff's dead and there's no point in stirring up a local scandal . . ."

"And you, Lash. Sam Carter was working for you?"

"I didn't kill the sheriff," Lash said quickly.

"Who did?"

"The man whose body was found with the sheriff's. A man named Harry Clyde."

"And who killed Clyde? The sheriff?"

"*I* didn't kill the sheriff," Lash repeated.

A little shiver seemed to run through Lieutenant Bailey. He said: "Well, that was in Illinois. About this Oliver Halpin . . . ?"

"You can take my word for it, he and his brother George haven't spoken to each other in more than thirty years. They hate each other's guts."

The lieutenant stared at Lash a

moment, then his eyes fell again to the book in his hand. "But about this book . . . ?"

"Halpin's a rich man. When he was a boy his mother gave a book like that to his cousin — she wrote her name in it. Well, Halpin wanted to locate that one particular book — the one his mother gave to his cousin . . . ."

"How old a man is Halpin?"

"Crowding sixty. The book was given to his cousin fifty years ago."

"Where's his cousin today?"

"He died forty-five years ago."

The lieutenant blinked. "And he wanted you to find this book that his mother gave to the kid cousin fifty years ago?"

"No — he'd *found* the book. He came in here with it."

The lieutenant exclaimed. "Now, wait a minute — I'm missing something here — he *had* the book and wanted you to find it . . . ?"

"No-no, he had the book, but he wanted me to trace it back to the original owner — to verify that this was the book his mother had given to his cousin, a boy named Stuart Billings."

"But you said, his mother had written her name in the book?"

"Correct, but he wanted to *prove* that this was his mother's handwriting."

"Didn't he know?"

"I'm telling you what Halpin *said* to me." Lash sighed. "I didn't say Halpin's story made sense, did I?"

Lieutenant Bailey glowered at Lash. "It's the screwiest thing I ever heard of." He drew a deep breath. "But look — this Sterling Knox hailed from Mt. Miller, Illinois — and so did Oliver Halpin. They were both here in Hollywood and one of them got murdered. It looks to me like — "

"Just a minute, Lieutenant, before you go making up your mind. There's another former Mt. Miller citizen mixed in this — a man named Claude Benton, who owns a little store in New York City, called Benton's Department Store."

Bailey winced. "I've heard of it. One of the biggest department stores in the country, isn't it?"

"I think it does a business of about a hundred million dollars a year."

"And Benton's mixed in this?"

"He was in Mt. Miller when I was there. He left a couple of hours before I did. Maybe he went back to New York and on the other hand, maybe he came here, to Hollywood . . ."

The lieutenant groaned. Then he suddenly looked at the warrant in his hand and thrust it back into his inside breast pocket. "I'm not going to do a thing, Lash, not until I talk to this Oliver Halpin."

He went to the door, opened it, then stopped.

"You're not figuring on taking any more trips, Lash?"

Lash shook his head. "No."

The lieutenant went out. Lash went to the bedroom window. He saw Bailey get into the police car, saw it pull off and saw a taxicab draw up into the spot vacated by the police car.

He returned to the library. "The door, Eddie," he announced, about one second before the buzzer whirred.

246

21

EDDIE went downstairs and returned with Oliver Halpin.

"I don't understand you at all, Lash," Halpin said as he came in. "For two days you refuse to talk to me, then suddenly you begin pulling your tricks — "

"Tricks, Mr. Halpin?"

"You know what I mean — telling my daughter the police want me."

"The car that pulled away just as you came up in the taxi — that was a police car. Lieutenant Bailey is on his way to your apartment, right now."

Halpin moistened his lips with his tongue. "You told him about me?"

"It was either that or go to jail. I told you I'd talk to the police if it came to a showdown. Well, that was the showdown."

"I thought a private detective kept a man's confidence," Halpin whined. "Like a lawyer, or — or — "

247

"A priest?" Lash suggested. His lips curled. "Mr. Halpin, I haven't been hiding the last two days. I've been to Mt. Miller, Illinois."

"What were you doing there?" Halpin cried.

"I sent a man there, first — a man from Chicago," Lash said, bluntly. "He was murdered — his body thrown into your brother's bull pasture, where it was trampled and gored by a bull."

Halpin's eyes threatened to pop from his forehead. "W-who — who would do a thing like that?"

"The sheriff," Lash said.

"Walters!" cried Halpin. "Why, I've known him all my life."

"Walters and his nephew, Harry Clyde," Lash said, "and then they shot each other."

Halpin reeled as if struck. "This — this all started because I — I asked you to trace down a measly book!"

"It started fifty years ago," Lash said.

"What?"

"I'm laying the cards on the table, Mr. Halpin," Lash said. "That book you brought up here — don't tell me

248

you didn't know there was a message in it — words underlined in pencil . . . "

Halpin walked to Lash's red leather couch and seated himself heavily. For a long moment he looked at Lash, then shook his head. "Yes," he said, dully, "I saw those underlined words. But — they didn't mean anything."

"Didn't they?"

"No. Somebody marked those words — for a game. Or for no reason at all."

"Who?"

"I don't know. The book is fifty years old — it's had a lot of owners."

"Oh, not so many. Stuart Billings, Claude Benton, his son, Charles Benton, Jay Monahan — you . . . "

"Me?"

"You brought me the book."

"I thought you meant — " Then Halpin caught himself.

"Mr. Halpin," Lash said slowly, "who is your cousin, Paul?"

Halpin squinted at Lash. "That's the thing that's been driving me crazy, Lash. I don't know. I never had a cousin named Paul. I never had any relative named Paul. That — that's why I came

to you. I wanted you to trace the book
— well, I *hoped* that someone along
the line who had owned the book had
a cousin named Paul. But . . . " His
words trailed off.

"What about the Bentons?" Lash
asked. "Any Pauls in their family?"

"Claude Benton was an only child.
There were no Pauls in his family . . . "

"Or his wife's? Charles Benton could
have a cousin named Paul, on his
mother's side."

"Maybe, but . . . Charles Benton is
alive. He wasn't murdered . . . "

Lash looked thoughtfully at Halpin for
a moment. The dried-milk manufacturer
sat on the couch, his face haggard, his
eyes worried. Then Lash said: "Mr.
Halpin, you suggested that someone
might have underlined those words as
a joke — or for no reason at all. Only
you don't believe that; well, why don't
you believe it?"

For a moment Halpin wouldn't look at
Lash. Then he raised his eyes. "You've
been to Mt. Miller, Mr. Lash. Did you
— did you learn anything there about
my cousin, Stuart Billings?"

"He died all right, forty-five years ago. Of pneumonia, the paper said. It's a little late to verify the cause of the death."

"I know, but that wasn't — well, that wasn't what I was referring to." Halpin cleared his throat. "I — I meant about his circumstances."

"He was a pauper, is that what you mean?"

Halpin hesitated. "Yes."

"Yet his father had been the richest man in the county. Only he lost all his money in a railroad deal; is that what you meant?"

Halpin said slowly: "My father built a new dairy not so long after Stuart's death."

"You mean there were assets that nobody knew about — nobody but your father?"

"That's not a very pleasant thing to think about your father, is it? Even though he's been dead for a long time. I — I have a daughter, Lash. I'd hate to have her learn that her grandfather was a — a thief."

"But if Stuart died, your father was the next of kin. He would have inherited the money, anyway. Of course if he — helped Stuart die . . . "

"No!" cried Halpin.

"But that's what you're thinking."

Halpin got to his feet. He looked at Lash and drew a deep breath. "I'm going to forget the whole thing. Stuart Billings died forty-five years ago, my father thirty-seven. I'm sorry I ever started this business. But I'm going to drop it now."

"Maybe the police won't want to drop it," Lash said.

Halpin looked sharply at Lash.

"Sterling Knox was murdered," Lash went on. "Here in California. In Mt. Miller, Illinois, Sam Carter was murdered — and two other men met violent death."

"You said Walters and Clyde killed this man Carter. Then they killed each other."

"Clyde killed Walters," Lash said. "*I* killed Clyde."

"You!"

"They were going to kill me."

Halpin walked toward the door, his shoulders sagging. Lash let him get his hand on the knob, open the door. Then he said: "Mr. Halpin, how long is it since you've seen your brother?"

Halpin turned slowly. He gave Lash a long look, then turned back and went down the stairs. Eddie Slocum started after him to see that the street door was latched.

The phone on Lash's desk rang. He picked it up. "Lash talking."

"Simon," said the voice of Phil Appleton. "Claude Benton's registered here, all right. He's got a suite adjoining young Benton's."

"I'll be over in a half hour," Lash said. "Wait for me in the lobby."

He hung up and got his hat as Eddie Slocum re-entered the library. "Stick next to the phone, Eddie."

"Where'll you be?"

"The Hollywood-Wilshire."

Lash descended the stairs, opened the door and crossed the street to the Ford.

The Cross operator watched him approach.

"Hello," he said.

Lash said: "I'm going to run over and see the man who hired your agency — Charles Benton."

"Yeah?"

"Yeah. And you're going to follow me, anyway. So why don't you drive me there?"

"This ain't no taxi."

"If you insist, I'll pay you the regular taxi fare."

"G'wan," said the operator, "beat it."

Lash shrugged and began walking. He went a half block when the car began to follow. Lash slackened his pace and the car, crawling at its slowest speed, nevertheless caught up to him. Lash stopped and lit a cigarette and the car was compelled to stop.

Lash began walking again. At the corner of Sunset, he stopped, began retracing his steps. The Ford made a U-turn. When it completed the turn Lash again turned and headed back for the corner. He waited for the car to make a second U-turn and catch up to him. Then he called: "See what I mean?"

"You win," said the man in the car.

Lash opened the door and climbed in beside the private detective. "Hollywood-Wilshire Hotel, son."

The man grunted. "This is silly."

"Ain't it the truth?"

The driver turned right on Fairfax and began scooting across town. After they had passed Melrose, Lash said: "Who was it conked me on the head in my apartment — you or someone else?"

"I don't know what you're talking about."

"I'm talking about the night somebody swiped a book from my place and I came in too soon — remember?"

"You're screwy."

"All right, skip it — for now."

On Wilshire the private detective turned right and a moment later pulled up in front of the Hollywood-Wilshire Hotel. Lash opened the door on his side.

"Do you have to go up with me, or are you just supposed to find out where I go?"

"Look, Mister," the private detective said angrily, "I don't know what you're talking about."

"All right, act as dumb as you look. But if you are coming in, I'll be in Charles Benton's room. Okay?"

The man made no reply and Lash went

into the lobby. Phil Appleton was playing the pinball game near the cigar stand. Lash crossed to him. "Charles is in eight hundred and six — his old man, eight hundred and eight; the rooms adjoin."

"What about phone calls?"

"He calls the Cross Agency about six times a day."

"And long distance?"

"He made a long distance call to Mt. Miller, Illinois, yesterday and he got one from there. And he's called Las Vegas, Nevada, a couple of times."

"What about other local calls?"

Appleton took a slip of paper from his pocket. There were four notations on it. One was Simon Lash's own telephone number. The other three were the same: Granite 1–5115.

"This Granite number . . . " Lash began.

"I thought you'd want to know. I called it. Somebody who answered, said, Oro Grande Apartments."

"Good," said Lash. "You're earning your money, Phil."

"I always do."

"I brought a man from the Cross

Agency over here with me — he looks like a gigolo, dark, long sideburns. He may come into the hotel in a minute. If he goes upstairs, you follow him."

Appleton nodded and Lash went to the elevators. "Eight," he said, as he stepped into a car.

A moment later he stepped out on the eighth floor and found 806 nearby. But he continued on to 808. He listened at the door and heard a rumble of voices, but could not distinguish words.

He knocked.

"Yes?" called a voice inside.

Lash tried the door, found it open and pushed into the room. Charles Benton was seated in an arm chair in an attitude of disgust. His father was pacing the floor. It was apparent that the elder Benton had been lecturing his son.

Both reacted in astonishment as Lash came into the room.

"Simon Lash!" cried Benton, senior. "I thought you were — "

"I left Mt. Miller two hours behind you," Lash said grimly. "You heard what happened there?"

Claude Benton hesitated. He had

heard, all right, but was trying to make up his mind as to whether he should admit it. Charles Benton cut in:

"You get around, Lash!"

"So do you. By the way — I rode over with the man from the Cross Agency."

Benton, Junior, gasped. "Who?"

"The man who's supposed to shadow me."

Claude Benton fixed his son with a cold stare. "Is that some other nonsense you haven't told me about?"

"I don't know what he's talking about," Charles Benton snapped.

"I'm talking about the day and night shift you've got on me, Benton," Lash snapped. "And I'm also talking about the man you had break into my place — the one who slugged me and stole the copy of *Ralph Raymond's Heir* . . . "

"You're crazy!" cried Charles Benton.

"I'll lay you a hundred dollars to a dime you've got the book right here in your place."

A slight gleam of triumph came to Charles Benton's face, but he erased it quickly. "I'll take that bet."

But Claude Benton was not satisfied.

"Charlie," he said warningly, "I want the truth; did you . . . uh, do that?"

"No," Charles Benton replied. "I haven't seen that Alger book."

Lash said sarcastically, "And you didn't hire the Cross Agency to shadow me?"

Young Benton hesitated, then shrugged. "I'll admit *that*."

"You're a fool, Charlie!" the older Benton said.

"I wasn't doing it for myself," Charles Benton retorted.

Lash said quietly to the elder Benton: "Don't you think it's about time we had a talk, Mr. Benton?"

"No," Claude Benton replied promptly. "I haven't got anything to talk about."

"We could talk about the murder of Sterling Knox."

"I wasn't in California when he was killed."

"Charles was . . . "

Charles Benton took a couple of quick steps toward Lash. "Why, you cheap flatfoot, I'll knock — "

"Knock ahead," Lash invited, "if you feel lucky."

At that Benton might have taken

a chance, but his father stepped in between the younger men. "There'll be no brawling. Charles, sit down. And you, Lash, get to hell out of here."

Lash sighed. "You may change your mind about talking."

"If I do I'll let you know."

Lash sighed, said: "But you were in Illinois when Sam Carter was murdered."

Benton regarded him dourly. "Get out!"

Lash left the room, rode down in the elevator and found Phil Appleton still playing the pinball game. About twenty feet away, the swarthy Cross operator sat in a big leather chair, reading the evening edition of the Los Angeles *Times*.

Lash went up to him. "Better call your office in about fifteen minutes," he said. "I think you'll be fired by that time."

The operator sneered. "Yeah?"

Lash went toward Phil Appleton. "Keep him from following me," he said as he walked by.

At the door Lash shot a quick

glance over his shoulder. The Cross man was coming toward the door. But Phil Appleton was cutting across to intercept him. Lash smiled and left the hotel.

22

OUTSIDE, he had the doorman signal for a taxicab and when it came he climbed in. "Oro Grande Apartments," he said.

"Where's that?" asked the cabdriver.

"Orange, just off Sunset."

Ten minutes later he paid off the taxicab in front of the dingy old mansion that had been converted into apartments. He entered the lobby and found it lighted by a twenty-five watt bulb, which gave just enough light to conceal the names on the mailboxes.

The first floor had produced only abuse the last time Lash had been here, so he climbed the stairs to the second floor where another twenty-five watt bulb gave forth a sickly light.

He knocked on the first door. It was opened by a hulking man who hadn't shaved for at least four days. Lash said: "I'm looking for Nell Benton."

"A guy can lose a lot of teeth knocking

on doors at ten o'clock at night and asking for a dame," snarled the man without the shave.

"I wouldn't be surprised," Lash said, "only I'm not looking for a dame — I'm looking for Nell Benton."

"Try the next door and if a man answers, duck." And with that the door was slammed in Lash's face.

A thread of light showed under the next door. Lash walked up to it, listened a moment, then knocked gently. Footsteps slithered on carpeting inside the room, then Nell Benton asked nervously: "Yes?"

"Simon Lash."

Lash could hear her inhale sharply. Then she said: "Please go away."

"Open up," Lash said.

"Go away," she repeated. "Go away, or I'll call the police."

"If I go away, *I'll* call the police."

There was another pause, then a chain rattled and Nell Benton opened the door a couple of inches. Lash pushed on it. She resisted, but was no match for him and suddenly stepped clear.

Lash entered the room and closed the

door. Her eyes widened in fright. "Please open the door."

"I want to talk to you," Lash said. "About your husband."

"My husb — " she began, then caught herself. "I haven't got a husband. I — I've been divorced."

"Then let's talk about your ex-husband. I've just come from him."

She backed away. "H-he sent you here?"

Lash looked about the one-room apartment. It contained a studio couch, a dressing table and a couple of chairs. "He wants the book," he said, bluntly.

Her head began to swivel, before she caught herself. "What book?"

Lash nodded toward the dresser beside the studio couch. "The one you've got there."

"I haven't got — I mean, the only book I've got is a novel from the rental library."

Lash started deliberately toward the dresser, but she headed him off. "I want the book," he said.

"I told you I haven't got it. I mean — I . . . "

Lash reached for the top dresser drawer. She grabbed his arm in both of her hands, tried to pull it away. But Lash let her wrestle with his arm, and half turning forced her away and with his left hand pulled open the dresser drawer.

The Alger book lay on top of some underclothing. He took it out and then Nell Benton let go of his arm and, retreating to the studio couch, seated herself heavily.

"All right," she said, dully, "take it and go."

"Who got the book for you?"

"What difference does it make?"

"Actually, none, but I'm curious."

"Let's say a friend, then. You wouldn't know him."

"Does he know why you wanted this book?"

She looked up at him. "I don't see . . . " Then she stopped. "What do you mean?"

"I mean," Lash said deliberately, "does this friend know you wanted this book because you're in love with your ex-husband?"

That brought her to her feet. "Love

Charles Benton?" she cried. "That conceited, spoiled, good-for-nothing — "

"Brat," said Lash. "And you talked to him three times yesterday."

She gasped. "How do you know?"

"I know something else," Lash said. "I know that Charles Benton would do almost anything in the world to get this book. He would even . . . marry you."

The color faded from her face. "You don't know what you're talking about!"

"He called you three times — you tried to bargain with him. But you can't bargain with a man like Charles Benton. He was born with a platinum rattle in his hand and he probably never felt a razor strop in his life. As you said, he's a conceited, spoiled brat. But you want him just the same, don't you?"

Her mouth opened to deny it, but no words came forth.

Lash said: "He isn't worth it."

Knuckles rapped on the door. A voice called: "Nell?"

"Oh!" gasped Nell Benton.

"Come in," Lash called.

The door was slammed open and a man who almost filled the doorway

266

appeared. He was about thirty, stood well over six feet and was built like a big fullback.

He looked at Lash and said: "This your husband, Nell?"

"Quick on the uptake, son," Lash said. He held up the Alger book. "I just stopped in to pick up the book you borrowed from me, the other night."

"Walter!" exclaimed Nell Benton.

But Walter was coming forward, walking on the balls of his feet.

Lash said, "Don't!"

Walter grinned wickedly. He made a pass at Lash's face and, as Lash's hands went up instinctively, he drove his fist into Lash's stomach.

Lash gasped in agony and bent forward. Then Walter's big fist exploded on his chin and he went careening back. He collided with Nell Benton and ricocheted from her to the studio couch. He crashed back on it and lay still for a moment, as he fought nausea.

He licked it after a moment and sat up, with an effort. Nell Benton was struggling to hold back Walter — and succeeding, since the young giant had already vented his rage on Lash.

Then he saw Lash sitting up. "I've got some more for you."

Lash said weakly: "You can lick me, but you're licked yourself. By a man who didn't even lay a finger on you. Charles Benton."

Walter took a step forward, then stopped and peered into Nell's face. Evidently he saw the confirmation there, for his huge body seemed to deflate as if punctured.

"Is that right, Nell?" he asked.

"No!" cried Nell.

"Yes," said Lash. "By this time tomorrow they'll be looking for a Justice of the Peace."

"So you're going back to him," Walter said thickly.

And then Nell could deny it no longer. She backed away from Walter, buried her face in her hands and began to sob.

Walter looked down at her from his superior height, swallowed hard and dropped a hand on her shoulder. "All right, Nell, if that's what you want."

He stepped back, exhaled heavily and

looked at Lash. "I don't know how, but you did it. The guy's no good, but if she wants him . . . " He shrugged wearily and went out, closing the door behind him. But he opened it again.

"Only you can tell him that there's a guy waiting for her. When she walks out on him the second time, I'll be there — and that's the last he'll see of her. Tell him that, for Wally Wayne."

He closed the door again. Lash heard heavy footsteps walk away and got to his feet. He felt rocky.

Nell raised a tear-stained face. "Please go," she said.

Lash nodded. "I'm taking this book with me, but don't worry."

He opened the door, stepped out into the hall. Twenty feet away, Wally Wayne stood in an open doorway. He was lighting a cigarette.

Lash said: "Sorry, chum."

Wally made no reply and Lash descended to the first floor. He stepped outside, went down the three short steps to the sidewalk and Clare Halpin came out of the shadows and fell in beside him.

"Mr. Lash, I saw you go in and I waited."

"When did you see me go in?"

"Ten minutes ago."

"You were watching the house out here?"

She nodded. "I — I was trying to get up nerve to go in to see Nell Benton."

"Why should you have to nerve yourself up to see her? You went to school with her."

"Yes, but . . . " She took Lash's elbow. "Please come with me. I want to talk to you. It's — very important."

Lash shrugged his elbow from her grip. "I'm not in the mood for talking tonight. Not any more. I'm going home."

A street light flashed on a stubby automatic in Clare Halpin's hand. Lash groaned. "For the love of — "

"There's my car," Clare Halpin said tautly. "Get into it." And as Lash remained still, "I mean it — you've had my father arrested and I could kill you for that."

"Your father's arrested?"

"They telephoned him and he went down and hasn't returned."

270

"The police didn't telephone your father. *I* called him. He came to see me."

"When?"

"More than an hour ago."

"He hasn't returned home."

She stabbed the automatic into Lash's ribs and he moved toward a coupe parked a few yards away. He opened the door on the curb side and she nudged him in the side again with the gun. "You drive."

He slid across behind the wheel, found the ignition key and turned it. Clare Halpin crossed her right hand in front of her, so that the automatic was pointed at Lash.

"Drive," she ordered.

"Where to?"

"Las Palmas."

"Your apartment?"

"Yes."

Lash pressed the starter button, and the motor caught at once.

He shifted into second gear and drove to Sunset, a short distance away. There he turned left. At Highland Avenue a motorcycle policeman was parked at the curb, waiting for speeders to beat the lights. Lash waited for the lights to change, then crossed Highland and went two blocks to Las Palmas, where he turned left.

He pulled up before the Santa Ana Apartments and shut off the ignition.

A doorman stepped up and opened the door on Clare's side. "Good evening, Miss Halpin," he said.

Clare stepped out and waited for Lash. Her hands were thrust into the pockets of her mink coat.

Lash got out on the street side and walked around the car. He smiled brightly at Clare Halpin and took her right arm — where her hand, down in the pocket, gripped the little gun.

"Well, here we are, darling," he said mockingly.

"Come in," she replied tensely.

"Why, of course," Lash replied easily. He let his hand slide down her forearm into her pocket. Her fingers resisted, but she was afraid of attracting attention and surrendered the gun.

As they passed through the small foyer, into the lobby, Lash transferred the automatic to his trousers pocket.

They crossed the lobby to the elevators, Lash still holding to her arm.

But when they got out on the fifth floor and the elevator doors closed on them, Clare Halpin tore her arm free of Lash's grip. "Give me that gun," she exclaimed.

Lash took it out, slipped out the clip of cartridges and handed her the gun. "Here you are, darling."

She walked stiffly to the door of an apartment, brought out a key and unlocked the door. Lash, close behind, reached past her and, turning the knob, pushed open the door.

Oliver Halpin looked at them in the mirror over the mantelpiece. He was standing before a fireplace in which a log fire burned — a gas log fire.

"Lash!" he cried, then stared at his daughter. "Clare, when did you . . . ?"

"Oh, we're old friends," said Lash.

"That's a lie," blazed Clare Halpin.

"Lash," said Halpin, "the biggest mistake I ever made in my life was going up to your office."

"Personally," retorted Lash, "I wish I'd never seen you."

Then Halpin saw the book in Lash's coat pocket. "Is that — *Ralph Raymond's Heir?*"

"Yes. I finally got it back."

"Who had it?"

Lash shrugged. "What's the difference?" He took the book from his pocket.

Halpin came forward, hand extended to take the book. But Lash avoided his reach. "Just a minute."

He opened the book, turned a couple of pages and found the underlined words: '*This is poison* . . . "

"Give it to me," Halpin ordered.

Lash riffled pages again, found a second group of words, underlined. Then Halpin jerked the book out of his hands. "This finishes us. Get out, Lash."

"You're the third person who's ordered me out this evening," Lash said. "I forced myself on the other two, but I came here against my will. At the point of a gun."

Halpin's eyes went to his daughter's face. She exclaimed: "I — I didn't know what to think, Dad, when you went down to the police station and didn't return . . . "

"I wasn't at the police station, Clare."

"That's what he said. But — "

Lash said quietly: "You didn't come right home from my place, Halpin."

"I took a walk."

"Missing Lieutenant Bailey?"

Halpin shook his head. "I didn't miss him — he left here ten minutes ago."

"After you told him — nothing?"

"I told him all I knew."

A phone rang and Halpin's eyes went across the room to a little niche in the wall where a phone reposed. Clare started for it, but Halpin called: "I'll get it."

He crossed to the phone, picked it up. "Yes?" Lash, all the way across the room saw Halpin react. Then Halpin said into the phone. "Tell them I'm out." He slammed the receiver back on the hook.

"You can't tell the police you're out," Lash said.

"That wasn't the police." Halpin snapped. "Not that it's any of your business. And, as for you, Lash, I said that we were through."

"Not quite. We made a deal. You wanted me to trace the original owner of this book. Well, I did."

"That's open to dispute, but I don't care to argue the point. Say you did what you agreed. All right, that ends your job. Good-bye . . . "

"After you pay me."

Halpin's eyes narrowed. "I gave you five hundred dollars."

"I've spent more than that. I asked you how high you'd go — you said money was no object."

"You're being ridiculous, Lash. Or" — Halpin's eyes narrowed — "you think you can shake me down!"

"Yes," said Lash. "Blackmail. It's been done before . . . "

Knuckles rapped peremptorily on the hall door. Halpin started visibly.

"I guess they didn't take no for an answer," Lash said.

23

THE knuckles rapped again — louder.

"Don't answer," Halpin said to his daughter, who was starting for the door.

If she heard him, she paid no heed. She went to the door, opened it. Lieutenant Bailey came into the room. Behind him were Claude and Charles Benton.

Bailey shook his head. "I know you told the clerk you didn't want to see them, Halpin, but I thought it'd be a good idea if we all got together and talked this thing out." He looked at Lash. "And you, Lash, I've got some embarrassing questions to ask you."

"You were down in the lobby when I came in?"

"Yep."

Claude Benton came into the room and walked up to Oliver Halpin. He looked him over carefully. "A long time, isn't it, Ollie?"

"I haven't missed you at all," Halpin retorted. He crossed to the mantel and put the Alger book on it. Then he turned.

"All right, let's get it over with."

Lieutenant Bailey looked at Lash. "I talked to Mr. Halpin this evening, Lash. His story didn't quite agree with yours."

"Naturally," Lash said. "As a matter of fact, Benton's story won't agree with Halpin's. And his story" — nodding at Benton, Junior — "won't agree with his wife's."

"What's my wife got to do with this?" Charles Benton cried.

"I just came from there," Lash said. "She's got a boy friend, named Wally Wayne — big handsome lad." He rubbed his chin ruefully. "With a wallop like a Missouri mule."

"So you walked into a couple. Well, when this is over, you're going to walk into some more."

"Cut it out, you two," growled Lieutenant Bailey. "Lash, I'm going to let you open the ball. You told me a cock-and-bull story about Mr. Halpin coming to you and wanting you to find the owner of a cheap Horatio Alger book. You stick to that story?"

"Has Halpin denied it?"

"Of course I have," Halpin snapped.

"Oh," said Lash, "so we're perfect strangers, are we?"

Halpin glowered at Lash. "You're full of tricks, aren't you, Lash?" He stabbed a finger at Lieutenant Bailey. "Officer, I told you that this man tried to blackmail me. I want you to arrest him. I'll prefer charges."

"Go ahead," Lash said. "Prefer them." He smiled at Claude Benton. "I guess that means he'll prefer charges against you, too."

Benton's eyes narrowed to slits.

Lash turned to Bailey. "As a matter of fact, Lieutenant, this does concern blackmail."

"Go ahead," Bailey invited. "Tell your story — if you've got one. I've got a lot of time. I've got all night. But tell a good story, because when you get through, I'm going to take you along with me."

Lash crossed to the mantelpiece and took down the Alger book.

"This book, Lieutenant, tells about a

murder that took place forty-seven years ago." He shot a quick look at Oliver Halpin. "Mr. Halpin, please note I said forty-seven years ago — not forty-five."

"I don't give a damn what you say, Lash," Halpin said. "I'm not even listening to you."

"Good — then I'll talk for the Lieutenant's benefit." Lash raised the cover of the book and held it so that Bailey could see the inscription on the fly-leaf. "Mr. Halpin's mother gave this book to her nephew, Stuart Billings, on his eleventh birthday, February second, eighteen ninety-seven. A nice gift, too, as the book cost a dollar and a quarter, which was a day's pay for a man in those days. And Mrs. Halpin wasn't rich, or even well-to-do. In fact, the family was quite poor." Lash looked inquiringly at Oliver Halpin, but the latter only scowled. He turned to Claude Benton. "You were poor then, too, Mr. Benton?"

Benton also remained silent.

Lash drew a deep breath and resumed: "Of course it didn't hurt to stand in with a rich man, for Stuart Billings' father

280

was the richest man in the county. He was even president of the local bank, which probably held a mortgage on the Halpin farm. And Mr. Billings, Senior, appreciated the friendship of his sister-in-law — and her family. Because when he lost his money a little while later — in a railroad deal — and took his own life, he left a will in which he appointed Mr. Halpin, Senior, the guardian of his son, Stuart."

Lash paused and looked carelessly at Oliver Halpin. "Only Mr. Billings didn't die by his own hand. He was murdered . . ."

Oliver Halpin's head came up so sharply that it almost cracked the mantelpiece behind him. "What's that?" he cried.

"Ralph Billings was murdered by *your* father . . ."

Lash held up the Alger book. "This book threw me, Halpin. It's inscribed to Stuart Billings and I assumed because it was his book that *he* had underlined the words. But when Stuart died he didn't have the book any more. In fact, he hadn't seen it for two years." He turned to Claude Benton. "Mr. Benton, you were living in Mt. Miller when Ralph Billings died. But two years later, when his son, Stuart, died, you'd already left Mt. Miller — gone to Chicago to make your fortune."

Claude Benton stared at Lash. "That's right," he said tonelessly.

"Dad," interrupted Charles Benton, "let's get out of here. We don't have to listen to this . . . "

Claude Benton crossed to a chair and seated himself. "Go ahead, Lash," he said.

"This book," Lash continued, "you had it in your possession for years. Your son got it — and he had it with him when he went to the Hudson Military Academy, where he shared a room with Richard Monahan, the actor's son. Charlie — you said Dick Monahan stole this book from you. Is that right?"

Charles Benton looked at his father. The latter nodded for him to answer. "Yes," snapped Charles Benton. "We had a fight and he got another room. I didn't know he took the book with him, but since it turned up in his possession, I

282

guess he took it, all right. I know I didn't *give* it to him."

Lash addressed Benton, Senior, again: "Mr. Benton, have you recalled yet just how you came into possession of this book?"

Benton sighed. "You've asked me that question several times. I told you that I couldn't remember. I suppose I did get the book from Stuart Billings . . . "

"On one of your rare visits to his home?"

Benton shrugged. "If you want to, you can say that I picked it up at the time of his father's funeral — which was the last time I was in his house."

"At any rate, you had the book when you left Mt. Miller?"

"Yes."

Lash looked at Lieutenant Bailey. "Make a note of that, Lieutenant — it's important."

Bailey bared his teeth. "Oh, sure!"

Lash ignored the sarcasm. "Mr. Benton, how long did you have this book before you discovered the underlined words in it — the words that told about the murder of Ralph Billings?"

"Ten years."

"What were you doing at the time?"

"I was working in a dry goods store in Chicago."

"And then you quit your job and bought a store of your own?"

Benton looked at the pattern on the carpet for a moment. Then he raised his eyes. "Yes, I got ten thousand dollars from Oliver Halpin. I — I blackmailed him for it."

"Dad!" cried Charles Benton.

"Now, now," Lash said chidingly to Charles Benton. "You've known it all the time. Otherwise, would you have hired someone to steal the book from me?"

Claude Benton looked steadily at his son. "Is that right, Charles?"

Charles Benton hesitated then nodded. "Yes, Dad, I — I came across it when I was twelve years old. I always wondered about it and a few years ago, I — well, I investigated."

"And you told your wife about it, too," Lash said.

Claude Benton sighed wearily. "I got my start by blackmailing a man."

"Ten thousand dollars, Dad," cried

Charles Benton. "But you ran it up to ten million."

"And I never enjoyed a dollar of it," Claude Benton said dully.

Lieutenant Bailey came forward. "That's water over the dam. It happened forty-fifty years ago, in Illinois. But a man was killed here in Hollywood, two nights ago, and I haven't heard a word about that."

Halpin said harshly: "Tell him, Lash." He went to a chair and seated himself heavily.

Lash looked at him sharply, then turned to Bailey. "Halpin made three million dollars in the dried-milk business. He retired and came to California. And then he saw Sterling Knox on the street."

"Coming out of a bookstore," Halpin interposed.

Lash nodded. "Sterling Knox had a daughter named Nell, who married a spoiled brat" — he glanced at Charles Benton — "named Charles Benton. For that alone Halpin hated Knox. But he was afraid of him because he didn't know how much Knox had learned — through

285

his daughter — from the Bentons. He took a room at the Lincoln Hotel and there he intercepted Knox's mail and found out that a book dealer had a book for Knox. Halpin got the book — and it turned out to be the one that had been held over his head for almost all of his life . . . "

"And Benton hadn't had the book for twenty years!" Halpin said bitterly.

"Only you had to be certain that this was the right book," Lash said. "That's why you came to me. But to make sure that I wouldn't tumble, you underlined a few additional words — about a cousin Paul being the murderer. That was to throw me off the track, in case I got too much information, wasn't it, Mr. Halpin?"

Halpin said, "You're telling it, Lash."

"Night before last," Lash went on, "you got a call from Sheriff Walters of Mt. Miller, Illinois — from a neighboring town, I guess. He told you that a private detective was in town, digging into the histories of the Halpin, Billings and Benton families. You made certain financial arrangements with him . . . "

"Damn you, Lash," Halpin said, thickly. "If you hadn't gone to Sterling Knox he'd be alive today." He paused. "And so would I . . . "

A spasm of pain contorted his face. Lash took a step forward, peered into Halpin's face, then whirled to Bailey.

"Call an ambulance!"

Bailey exclaimed. "Poison . . . !" He headed for the phone. As he whipped off the receiver, Halpin called to him. "They'll be too late. I took it ten minutes ago."

Halpin was right. He was dead before the ambulance arrived.

★ ★ ★

Some time later the Bentons and Lash left the apartment. Outside the apartment house, Charles Benton gripped Lash's arm. "All right, Lash," he said ominously, "you made some cracks about my wife . . . "

Lash hit him three times, once in the face, once in the stomach and then a second time in the face.

Benton went down to the sidewalk

and as he sat there, looking up stupidly, Lash said:

"I'm going to call on your wife tomorrow afternoon," he said, "and if you haven't been there by that time and begged her to take you back I'm going to look you up and what you've just had isn't even going to be a sample of what you'll get . . .'"

Claude Benton said, "And I'm going to stand in line and take over after you finish with him, Lash."

Lash walked away from them.

THE END

FATAL RING OF LIGHT
Helen Eastwood

Katy's brother was supposed to have died in 1897 but a scrawled note in his handwriting showed July 1899. What had happened to him in those two years? Katy was determined to help him.

NIGHT ACTION
Alan Evans

Captain David Brent sails at dead of night to the German occupied Normandy town of St. Jean on a mission which will stretch loyalty and ingenuity to its limits, and beyond.

A MURDER TOO MANY
Elizabeth Ferrars

Many, including the murdered man's widow, believed the wrong man had been convicted. The further murder of a key witness in the earlier case convinced Basnett that the seemingly unrelated deaths were linked.

THE WILDERNESS WALK
Sheila Bishop

Stifling unpleasant memories of a misbegotten romance in Cleave with Lord Francis Aubrey, Lavinia goes on holiday there with her sister. The two women are thrust into a romantic intrigue involving none other than Lord Francis.

THE RELUCTANT GUEST
Rosalind Brett

Ann Calvert went to spend a month on a South African farm with Theo Borland and his sister. They both proved to be different from her first idea of them, and there was Storr Peterson — the most disturbing man she had ever met.

ONE ENCHANTED SUMMER
Anne Tedlock Brooks

A tale of mystery and romance and a girl who found both during one enchanted summer.

CLOUD OVER MALVERTON
Nancy Buckingham

Dulcie soon realises that something is seriously wrong at Malverton, and when violence strikes she is horrified to find herself under suspicion of murder.

AFTER THOUGHTS
Max Bygraves

The Cockney entertainer tells stories of his East End childhood, of his RAF days, and his post-war showbusiness successes and friendships with fellow comedians.

MOONLIGHT
AND MARCH ROSES
D. Y. Cameron

Lynn's search to trace a missing girl takes her to Spain, where she meets Clive Hendon. While untangling the situation, she untangles her emotions and decides on her own future.

NURSE ALICE IN LOVE
Theresa Charles

Accepting the post of nurse to little Fernie Sherrod, Alice Everton could not guess at the romance, suspense and danger which lay ahead at the Sherrod's isolated estate.

POIROT INVESTIGATES
Agatha Christie

Two things bind these eleven stories together — the brilliance and uncanny skill of the diminutive Belgian detective, and the stupidity of his Watson-like partner, Captain Hastings.

LET LOOSE THE TIGERS
Josephine Cox

Queenie promised to find the long-lost son of the frail, elderly murderess, Hannah Jason. But her enquiries threatened to unlock the cage where crucial secrets had long been held captive.

THE TWILIGHT MAN
Frank Gruber

Jim Rand lives alone in the California desert awaiting death. Into his hermit existence comes a teenage girl who blows both his past and his brief future wide open.

DOG IN THE DARK
Gerald Hammond

Jim Cunningham breeds and trains gun dogs, and his antagonism towards the devotees of show spaniels earns him many enemies. So when one of them is found murdered, the police are on his doorstep within hours.

THE RED KNIGHT
Geoffrey Moxon

When he finds himself a pawn on the chessboard of international espionage with his family in constant danger, Guy Trent becomes embroiled in moves and countermoves which may mean life or death for Western scientists.

TIGER TIGER
Frank Ryan

A young man involved in drugs is found murdered. This is the first event which will draw Detective Inspector Sandy Woodings into a whirlpool of murder and deceit.

CAROLINE MINUSCULE
Andrew Taylor

Caroline Minuscule, a medieval script, is the first clue to the whereabouts of a cache of diamonds. The search becomes a deadly kind of fairy story in which several murders have an other-worldly quality.

LONG CHAIN OF DEATH
Sarah Wolf

During the Second World War four American teenagers from the same town join the Army together. Forty-two years later, the son of one of the soldiers realises that someone is systematically wiping out the families of the four men.

THE LISTERDALE MYSTERY
Agatha Christie

Twelve short stories ranging from the light-hearted to the macabre, diverse mysteries ingeniously and plausibly contrived and convincingly unravelled.

TO BE LOVED
Lynne Collins

Andrew married the woman he had always loved despite the knowledge that Sarah married him for reasons of her own. So much heartache could have been avoided if only he had known how vital it was to be loved.

ACCUSED NURSE
Jane Converse

Paula found herself accused of a crime which could cost her her job, her nurse's reputation, and even the man she loved, unless the truth came to light.

BUTTERFLY MONTANE
Dorothy Cork

Parma had come to New Guinea to marry Alec Rivers, but she found him completely disinterested and that overbearing Pierce Adams getting entirely the wrong idea about her.

HONOURABLE FRIENDS
Janet Daley

Priscilla Burford is happily married when she meets Junior Environment Minister Alistair Thurston. Inevitably, sexual obsession and political necessity collide.

WANDERING MINSTRELS
Mary Delorme

Stella Wade's career as a concert pianist might have been ruined by the rudeness of a famous conductor, so it seemed to her agent and benefactor. Even Sir Nicholas fails to see the possibilities when John Tallis falls deeply in love with Stella.

CHATEAU OF FLOWERS
Margaret Rome

Alain, Comte de Treville needed a wife to look after him, and Fleur went into marriage on a business basis only, hoping that eventually he would come to trust and care for her.

CRISS-CROSS
Alan Scholefield

As her ex-husband had succeeded in kidnapping their young daughter once, Jane was determined to take her safely back to England. But all too soon Jane is caught up in a new web of intrigue.

DEAD BY MORNING
Dorothy Simpson

Leo Martindale's body was discovered outside the gates of his ancestral home. Is it, as Inspector Thanet begins to suspect, murder?